ANTIQUITY

a novel

Hanna Johansson

Translated from the Swedish by

Kira Josefsson

Catapult  New York

ANTIQUITY

This is a work of fiction. All of the characters, organizations, and events portrayed in this novel are either products of the author's imagination or are used fictitiously.

Antiken © Hanna Johansson, first published by Norstedts, Sweden, in 2020
Published by agreement with Norstedts Agency
Translation copyright © 2024 by Kira Josefsson

The cost of this translation was supported by a subsidy from the Swedish Arts Council, gratefully acknowledged.

First Catapult edition: 2024

ISBN: 978-1-64622-171-4

Library of Congress Control Number: 2023943115

Jacket design by Nicole Caputo
Jacket photograph © Maria Yakimova / Trevillion Images
Book design by tracy danes

Catapult
New York, NY
books.catapult.co

Printed in the United States of America

1 3 5 7 9 10 8 6 4 2

1.

❦ Persefonis ❦

FOR THREE DAYS ON THE SQUARE THEY'D been showing the world championships in harpoon fishing on a screen in front of the city hall. There was a stage for the competitors and a metal scaffolding that cast discs of sunlight on the functionaries as they bustled around in preparation for the evening. Day after day, the same order of events, like a ritual. There were white tents, tall tables, sponsor champagne and mineral water; there were loudspeakers and a winners' stand; there were lanterns being lit. When the sun came down, sailboats anchored in the harbor, and the men came with their sons. The men with taut stomachs and sunglasses atop their heads, the sons with bony knees, ruddy cheeks, thick hair, sad eyes. These were wealthy teens, dressed in sweatshirts and baggy swim trunks. They were well-mannered and bored. A vacation memory added to many others, to recollections of beach toys in white nets, Coca-Cola with slices of lemon and ice, calamari, french fries, seasickness, the brown bottle of Piz Buin sunscreen and the green bottle of aloe vera that came after.

The men took great interest in the events. The blue rectangle beneath the palm trees, the underwater footage, the fish weighed on the stage. The competition itself was underway elsewhere on the island, in the sea that lapped the rough beaches. On film the divers resembled gods with their harpoons and fit bodies, the wetsuits that made them smooth, nonhuman. They shone their flashlights into the underwater caves, making them look like crypts full of gold and precious stones.

The sons slouched listlessly over the tables. They took off, leaving their fathers; they bled onto the square, where they drifted around looking like they could use something to lean on; the handlebars of a bike, a fence outside of a school. They flung their arms about like they were waiting for someone to rough up or embrace. They were at the end of childhood and at the threshold of life, lonely with their impatient boredom, their painfully growing bodies, the final weeks of the summer at seaside bars, beaches, boats, and cafés, the taste of life's first coffee: lots of sugar, lots of foamed milk, like drinking sand.

The three of us were on the periphery, under the arches in the back. We were drinking white wine and Coca-Cola with slices of lemon and ice. We were seated so we could see the square, the stage, the screen, the crowd, and the city hall illuminated by spotlights. We stayed late; we stayed as the square emptied and the people returned to the harbor, to their sailboats and their hotels. We stayed as the functionaries cleared out the tables, the amps, and the winners' stand until all that was left was the scaffolding, bare and mute in the darkness, like a ruin.

WE WALKED HOME along the shoreline. Helena and Olga were ahead of me, arm in arm, complexly linked. Behind them I felt like a stranger, someone who had picked two people at random to trail, a menacing shadow. I walked like a watcher; I adapted to their pace. Helena and Olga had their names and their boundaries, mother and daughter, their roles and their particular duties, their story. I had nothing. I was a guest.

Helena walked on the side closest to the sea, like a keeper or a prison guard. The wine had made her slow and quiet.

Olga turned around and looked at me one single time during that walk by the sea, and I was scared at the thought of what she saw then, the look I gave her, lonely, caught in the act. I too was slow, quiet.

FOR THREE DAYS on the square—it was an image I kept coming back to. I kept returning to the square at night, I kept returning to this beginning of my story that was not a beginning.

It was not my summer. It was not my childhood.

It was a story I told myself, a memory I was preparing for later, one I hoped would give me much joy at some point, and much grief too. It was like the coast when you leave it, the coast seen from the stern of a boat, that last image: a point that recedes until you can no longer see it, until it is one with the horizon, a line drawn between before and after.

I was in the horizon. I was in the sea beneath the sun. I was on the square at night with the low, brown sky.

When I returned to that image, I pictured the uneven colonnade of the palm trees, not from below, but level with the tree crowns, as though I were a giant or a god.

IT WAS WARM on the square at night. It was warm on the seaside walk home. When we left Ermoupoli later it was fall, and I was cold. We sat on deck in the gusty dark; Olga was scared of falling overboard, of being snatched by the wind. Helena: don't be silly. But I understood her fear. There was nothing to separate sky and sea; the black was the black of cherries, it was like moving through time or through the void.

I was sitting between them. We were traveling toward the end and I was sick. I felt sick on the ferry. I felt like a stranger, distant. I fled into memory, or perhaps memory fled into me. I pictured myself and I saw a person for whom there was no hope. I had a first glimpse of the contours not of my death but of my life, the life I had lived up until that moment, the time and the experiences that had come to replace my dreams. A disappointment. I felt disappointed.

I pictured the pigeons taking off, the teens, the illuminated palm trees. I pictured an octopus swimming in the dark. It was not a real memory but it was just as real as a real memory, no different. I could hear my own voice narrating: the sun was so strong you always had to squint a little. I felt reality take its leave of me. I wasn't there.

Olga did not look at me. She looked straight ahead, hands in her pockets; she looked at the night, the deck, the water, which we could not see but which lay before us. Meaningless hours ahead: there was nothing to say. All that was left was the wait.

We were sitting outside even though it was cold. It was

Helena's idea. She wanted to be out on deck, it was wonderful, it was refreshing. Helena tried to say something and I couldn't hear; the noise drowned out her voice: the funnel, a vibration as though from an enormous flame somewhere. She had to yell: another time I'll show you the ruins at Delos, they're not going anywhere, they've been there for thousands of years already.

AT THE TIME of the world championships in harpoon fishing I'd been on Ermoupoli for a couple of weeks, the others for longer. Helena had gone there to rest. She called for me from the island, once I'd started getting used to the disappointment of being left behind, left out. But she had been mistaken, she needed me, and as so often in the course of our short friendship her regret gave me a renewed sense of power: it proved I was right. She asked me to come keep her company. The days were long, she was bored, she was feeling restless. She was feeling lonely. I let her believe I was mulling it over because I wanted to hear her say more. She could pay for my ticket—you'll have the best room; she sent pictures—you have to see it with your own eyes. I could stay for as long as I wanted. For weeks. As briefly as I wanted too—even a few days would be great. I negotiated through my silence. I accepted her invitation, an invitation I'd already fantasized about.

Olga had joined her because she was Helena's daughter. Olga needed no invitation; she came with Helena wherever she went, whether she wanted to or not.

EVEN BEFORE HELENA asked me to come I had spent a lot of time dreaming of this place, which I could initially only access through her stories. I imagined a city full of ruins, relics from the dawn of history. I pictured the city as a very peaceful place, fixed in a vague past. No cars. No sounds, no colors. Ermoupoli: a beautiful name, the city of Hermes, sharing its name with the place where Hadrian had the body of Antinous embalmed, the last place he saw in life, the place where he was idolized for his beauty and his youth, his link to death's deities. Ermoupoli, usually spelled with a rough-breathing diacritic: ʽE. A hint of a consonant, not quite a letter, just the sound of an aspiration: h.

All of this led me to assume it was an ancient city. But I soon learned that Ermoupoli was new, newer than Sweden, newer than the United States, founded in the war of independence in the early nineteenth century. A German architect built an expensive city hall in neoclassical style. The same architect designed the national theater and the presidential palace in Athens, hundreds of buildings across the country, a girls' school, a railway station, a villa on Vasilissis Sofias Avenue, which by the time I'd heard of it had already long been home to a museum of Cycladic art, full of marble figurines with crossed arms from all over the island nation, from its prehistory, that dusky, wordless time, like prelinguistic memory: to be born, to be breastfed, to open one's eyes. Ermoupoli was stately like Europe, and Europe was stately like ancient Greece. For a few decades the city had been home to the country's largest port, a stop for every steamship line between Europe and the Levant; a few decades of being a center, a place in the world, only to lose its importance again in the twentieth century, become periphery anew, a small city on an island in the Aegean. A period of greatness no longer than the lifespan of a human. It was a story that spoke to me.

After she told me that she was going to Ermoupoli with Olga to get away from everything, that she was going to stay for several weeks, perhaps months—it was in the summer, after she'd buried her father, and I remember that she told me when we were sitting outside somewhere even though it was cold, we were drinking dry martinis and I stabbed the olive with the little plastic spear, again and again while she talked—I often pictured her in her house at night, feet on a stool, a book, a glass of wine, for some reason I pictured a candle though in reality she probably had no need for one. I imagined her as very lonely in that house, and I wondered if she ever did feel lonely when she was there. It was difficult to fit the daughter in that picture, partly because I knew so little about her (I did not know exactly what she looked like, how she moved, what her voice sounded like, what her tastes were, and my fantasies of her were muddled, ever-changing; I pictured her sometimes as a child, sometimes as a grown woman) and partly because it was painful. Helena would not be lonely at all, since they had each other. The house too; it was just as difficult to picture the house. I didn't know the ways in which one room connected to another, whether the building was small or large, pale or dark, and whenever I lingered on that image of Helena at night—the stool, the book, the wineglass, the candle—the entire scene fell apart as soon I tried to tease out the details (what did the stool, the glass, the candlestick look like?) so that all that was left was the book on her knees, her hands, as if I were looking at them with her eyes.

Afterward, it would be impossible to revisit my initial fantasies about the city, about the house, about Olga. Reality took over and replaced my private dreams and I knew that memory, in turn, would soon distort reality. What had for many weeks appeared natural, immediate (the way to the sea, the precise feeling of slippery pavement under my feet, the sound of the bedroom door closing) would turn into fragments and reconstructions as new fantasies took the place of memory.

This began already on the departing ferry, in the darkness and the noise and the vibrations, my return to the nocturnal square, the image that had stuck, expanded, become mythical, overwhelming, and it made me feel very far from Helena and Olga though we were still close, though I was seated in between them. We could not see the horizon. It seemed like the world ended past the ferry lights, an end that was less a nothing and more a forever, a space in which we were moving with no destination. No change, nothing waiting to happen. The image of the square at night, the world championships in harpoon fishing, the arches and the palm trees and the men, these images that faded and came back into focus, they changed, they were the same. Certain aspects were the same. That image, it stayed with me for the duration of the long journey over. It was the last image of anticipation and uncertainty; call it innocence.

MY TRIP TO ERMOUPOLI had three legs to it. Two flights, one ferry ride. The first leg was before dawn, early enough that it was still dark out. It was drizzling when I left my home and the late-summer season was ice-cold, was green and black. The flashing light on the wings while I waited for the plane to take off: red. The purser demonstrating the safety routines, the oxygen mask, the life vest, the whistle had a beautiful voice in German and a gurgling, distraught voice in English. She sounded nervous, like she was about to cry. She told us there would be turbulence. We traveled through clouds that were like billowing smoke in the darkness, and the careening sounds of the airplane, the noise of the engine, and the flashing lights on the wings made the scene out my window look like a thunderstorm on a stage, King Lear on the heath. The overhead lights were turned off, and the man in the seat closest to mine was playing music from the phone he'd placed in his seat pocket, a translucent sound over the dull, incessant humming of the plane.

I washed my hands in Munich. A melody that brought to mind a self-playing piano was piped into the airport restroom and the floor was shiny, wet, fragrant of a cleaner that incongruously made the room appear unhygienic, grimy. Everything in there was square: the wide sinks in imitation marble, the tiles, the flimsy doors on the booths, the modern hand-driers that resembled ATMs where they hung on the walls. When I slipped my hands into the drier, the bathroom music was drowned out by the deafening sound of the fan, which was launched by my movement and which made the skin on my hands billow over my knuckles like waves. The drier made me uncomfortable; I hated the sound and the speed, the blue light that kept time and turned off when my hands, after just a few seconds, were entirely dry. I hated what it did to my hands: it made them look aged, bony, like I was old; it made them look like a sketch of my dead hands.

I was bored waiting for the next flight, which was headed to Athens. I felt impatient. I was expectant. I walked through the tax-free, the shiny shelves, opulent and tawdry, the rows of cigarettes, extra-large liquor bottles, the makeup's chunky packaging and the testers that were sticky from so many hands, an excess of everything. I sprayed on a little of Helena's perfume, Opium; she pronounced Yves Saint Laurent like an Englishwoman: Eve Sayn Laurang, I've worn the same thing since the eighties, I can't wear anything else, I wouldn't feel like myself.

I was tempted to put some on whenever I saw the bottle at her house in Stockholm, that red and gold, try her scent on me, become her a little bit. I liked the smell on her, on her clothes, spicy and balsamic in the apartment where it had settled. But at the airport, in her absence, it made me nauseous. It started out sharp, then it was stale, cloying. During what remained of the wait I had the feeling of being pursued, repeatedly catching a scent I could not identify; I felt it as if someone were nearby, right behind me, and I kept looking over my shoulder, confused and uncomfortable, only to realize it was just me.

Before the second leg, the middle leg, there was a last-minute change, and the Athens-bound plane was replaced by a much larger plane with more seats than passengers. I was assigned a number but told I could sit anywhere I liked. I had an entire row to myself, by the windows where frost bloomed above the clouds, in the far back, at a distance from the other passengers, who had spread out in the front.

Time shrank as distance grew. The subway ride to the harbor, the gray-and-white city, the vegetation, the dirty awnings, the journey underground, side by side with a time that was different but also mine, the history I'd been taught was the foundation of everything. Waiting for the ferry I stepped inside a church to cool off. A sign outside, in French and English, the languages of tourism: THIS IS A HOLY ROOM . . . To the side, a shop selling candles and incense, ORTHODOX CHURCH SUPPLIES, in English. I looked on as people entered and exited the space, kissed the icons, caressed the face of baby Jesus.

I'd been wearing a lot of clothes when I left. A sweater and a shirt, a heavy coat I normally used in the fall and which I would not touch during the weeks that followed in Ermoupoli, not until we left. I was sweaty, the skin sticky under my arms, sticky under my breasts, down my neck where my hair lay plastered. It was still warm when darkness fell over the sea. Approaching my destination I peeled off my layers— coat, sweater—and by the time I arrived, by the time the bow visor that separated the journey from the city opened, by then I was holding everything in my arms.

ERMOUPOLI HAD THE SHAPE of an amphitheater. The evening I arrived, when the ferry approached the harbor and I saw the city's lights emerge from the darkness, the buildings looked like streams of glowing lava. It was as if they had gushed out of the rock through two rifts, an audience before the stage that was the sea, a black stage set at night turned blue and white by the sun, an expanse that seemed to stretch until the end of the world.

On the night I arrived, Helena was waiting for me in the harbor. It took me a while to find her in the crush of people who were either disembarking or standing around before they could board and continue on to other islands, Mykonos, Naxos; I had a moment of panic (she wasn't there, I was in the wrong place, I had misunderstood something, I was alone) and excitement (fate had sent me to an unfamiliar place, I was on the brink of discovering something, I was alone); then I saw her and called her name. The light from the ferry made her face look green and oily, like wax. Her frizzy hair was loose, she was wearing slides, I noticed that her nails had grown long. She helped me with my things. She steered me away from the sea and to the stairs leading into the city, past the ferry office and the tourism agency, past the baskets of nougat and loukoumi, past a casino next door to a chapel, past a store for musical instruments and a schoolyard where the lights were on for nobody. She walked faster than me, her steps longer, wider.

It felt like it was our first time meeting, she was so polite, so nervous in her demeanor. As we climbed the stairs she told me that it was always surreal to receive guests since they were a reminder that this place was real, that it took up space in the consciousnesses of other people and not just hers, that it kept existing even when she wasn't there herself. It's a weird way of thinking, isn't it, she said, kind of like a child who believes she's invisible when she covers her eyes, I guess I'm a little childish. They hadn't had guests in a long while, she said. She couldn't even remember the last time—many years ago, many, many years ago. This was a shock: maybe she had changed her mind, but I couldn't know if the jolt of fear had to do with her or with me and the doubt that had always colored our interactions.

Helena came from a shipping family; that's why she walked like she owned the world. The man who had sold her the house, she told me, was a former shipyard worker, and this, she said, this was when I knew: it was a sign, this is where we were meant to be, it's a gift. Her daughter's happy childhood summers in the white light.

We got to Persefonis, the short street where Helena's house was wedged between an alley and a ruin, and she opened the unlocked door and led me through the darkened house, up an iron spiral staircase, walking so quietly as to be theatrical, like she was trying to make fun of herself and her effort to be quiet.

This daughter, my rival, who I had not yet met and who I'd never managed to picture in any clear or concrete way—I didn't meet her that night. She was in bed when we entered, sleeping behind a closed door on the top floor, where a narrow landing separated her room from mine.

I DIDN'T LIKE IT when Helena said "my daughter." I didn't like it when Helena said "Olga." The intimacy of speaking a name you've given someone. Later I learned that Olga's name actually came from her father's side, a family name that linked her to his lineage. But by then her name had come to hold associations entirely distinct from the ones I had in the beginning.

Olga, a name for the child of an artist. A name for a princess, a violent saint. A name for a little cunt.

I hated the name before I met her; I hated it when I only knew her by name, when all I knew was what Helena had told me about her. It stirred up feelings that made no sense in their forcefulness. A burning rage. A strange and inexplicable sensation of being left out. The beauty of the name embarrassed me. I hated her name because it was beautiful.

At night I spoke the name to myself, mouth closed. I tasted it on my own tongue, the tongue that whipped the palate over the *g* and turned it into a *k*, Olka, the *O* an aspiration. It was impossible to shape her name without a tiny impression of breath before the *O*, a whisper of the roots of the name: Helga, holy. Olga, soundless in my closed mouth, it was like swallowing hard.

I imagined the echo of it reaching her where she lay, haunting her dreams. I imagined that she, like me, lay awake listening to the sounds surrounding us, the cats, the nighttime ferry, the sea, the knowledge of another body moving in another bed in another room.

I was waiting for her then. I didn't know, but I was waiting.

I LEFT ONE SUMMER, and when I arrived in Ermoupoli another took over.

A couple of days before my departure I'd gone to see Josef dance in Vitabergsparken. The benches were cold and without give, it was crowded, I was alone. Afterward I saw that Helena had called me while my phone was off, that she'd messaged to say that she missed me, that it would be nice to have me near; she'd written: I can't manage without you.

I hadn't seen Josef in a long while. That summer he'd been left by Alain, Alain who pronounced his name Alayn and not Ala', which meant that the first time he said his name to Josef in Frankfurt, where they met, Josef had thought he said, in German, "I'm alone." Josef and I got a bottle of wine after his performance and we kept coming back to this origin story, which used to be comic but had become majestically romantic. He wanted Alain back so that he could leave him, on his own terms. He wanted closure. It was not a good summer.

Josef was preoccupied with his own aging, he was worried that his body would fail him, he felt he'd lost a lot of time because their relationship had ended, as if the breakup had erased the time they'd been together. He was furious with Alain, who had robbed him of his future dreams, his fantasies about growing old together. But we're not old, I said, and he said: I am, and in a way he was right. The chronology of his life was different from mine, a chronology of muscles.

When he danced the final of three short pieces in the park it was already dark. The spotlights were on and the stage resembled a glowing hearth in the dark, a campfire. The lights made him orange, the shadows long. He looked terrible, wounded, vanquished. Only I could see it, I was sure of that, and in that moment I savored the feeling of knowing him better than anybody else, despite everything, of seeing his emotions play across his body as if it were a map I'd marked with pins, on his face, his muscles, all the parts of him that I had conquered through the years.

And at the same time it was like watching a stranger. I saw him from the outside. I looked at him as I would look at something I had left behind.

I never liked Alain. I didn't like speaking English with him, I didn't like that he stole Josef from me, I didn't like that he made Josef sad. But now that he was out of the picture I felt abandoned and betrayed. I felt overwhelmed at the thought of being alone with Josef. I felt bad that I hadn't seen him in a long time and that I was about to go on a trip without him. I was angry with Alain because he had broken us up, the unit that the three of us had become, the only fixture in my life over the past several years, and in doing so had revealed that we weren't a unit at all, just three lonely people with their own stories to bear.

Josef and I got to know each other shortly before he met Alain, no more than a few months prior but still enough time to make me feel that he belonged to me primarily and that Alain was my rival. Our friendship often felt like a contest with rules only I knew but points only they could award. I loved that each of them discussed the other with me, that they confided in me, "but don't tell him I told you this." I loved knowing. And now my knowledge was useless.

When I left I had the feeling of taking off to never return

again, and in that moment it was a prospect that appealed to me: I wanted to change. Once again I was hoping to find my place, to find my place in the world at last, the one I'd been drifting around in search of for as long as I could remember. I readied myself to leave a part of me behind, a part that no longer seemed valuable.

Josef said: I'll miss you while you're in Greece, but I understood that he was already missing me, even as I was sitting right there across from him.

OVER THE PAST couple of years in the house on Persefonis, Helena had been sleeping in a small space on the ground floor next to the kitchen, a room previously used for storage, a supply closet, a place for stashing junk and random objects. She had developed insomnia but was scared of pills. She was plagued by night sweats and woke up soaked through and uneasy. This was going on before I met her, and sometimes I wondered how else she was different back then, what parts of her life I had missed, what our relationship would have looked like if we'd met earlier, if it would have been easier or more difficult; maybe it wouldn't have been possible at all.

In this new bedroom, narrow and austere, without a window and without room for anything but her bed, it was always dark and cool. She was no longer tormented by nighttime mosquitoes or aches or sounds; she slept, uninterrupted, until she woke. She called the room "the sarcophagus," inspired by a headline in a gossip magazine about the Danish queen whose husband did not want to be buried with her in the casket made of glass, Danish granite, Faroese basalt, and Greenland marble that had been constructed more than ten years earlier: ALONE IN THE SARCOPHAGUS. Alone in there, no man. Helena was fascinated by the casket, she loved stone, marble, she loved monuments, although she noted that she personally would never want to be buried in anything so precious and durable that it might inspire a future civilization to plunder her grave and exhibit the spoils at a museum. Once, she said, I saw this absolutely incredible thing at the archaeological museum—she lamented the fact that I'd never been, you should have gone while you were in Athens, she said, it sounded like a reprimand—what she'd come across was an inscription at the base of a soldier's pillar tomb, which read: The dead is fully armed. She ended the anecdote there. The subject made her uncomfortable and we moved on.

In the mornings, after breakfast, when she thought it was too hot to be outside, she'd stretch out on her bed and smoke in the dark, a saucer balanced on her stomach for an ashtray, and I tried, politely and without much enthusiasm, to make her stop so that the room wouldn't become her actual grave. She told me that smoking was the last indulgence she allowed herself, the only one she would not abstain from, as if to indicate that her personal history was full of bigger and riskier forms of decadence. She had planned to stop smoking altogether that summer but she'd changed her mind: smoking brought shape to a life; it meant you always had something to do. I didn't believe it when she called it her last indulgence because I knew she never denied herself anything, and it seemed, instead, that saying those words, "my last indulgence," was what brought her pleasure.

In my room, which used to be where she slept, the biggest of the bedrooms and facing the sea with a small balcony where I hung my towels to dry, the sun entered as soon as dawn broke.

Mornings were blinding, compact heat. At night there would often be a wind blowing from the sea, coming in from the east. The wind was in the palm trees on the square; the wind was in the fruit trees in Helena's garden. But on my side, the side facing the street and the stairs down to the harbor, the wind had nothing to take hold of; it just whined and sighed through the emptiness between the walls. Early in the morning, just before the sun, I would sometimes be woken by the sound of the sinkers that weighed down the balcony-door mosquito net hitting the floor.

As a child there was a game I'd play before falling asleep: I would pretend I was on a ship out at sea, and that the light from the cars that drove by outside, white crosses pulling over the floor, came from a lighthouse. I was reminded of this game as I lay in the unfamiliar room and the flat, artificial moonlight of a streetlamp fell in through the open door. Around midnight I'd hear the bow visor of the last ferry open with a plaintive noise, and in time the sound of the horn slowly faded from the harbor.

THE FIRST TIME I met Olga was in the garden, the morning after my arrival in Ermoupoli, but this wasn't the first time I saw her. Helena had shown me pictures. In real life she looked both older and younger than she did in these photos, the majority of which showed her as a child, a five-year-old, a four-year-old, in costume or with food smeared around her mouth—but those pictures still made me think of her as older than she was because they made me imagine her as someone who had been a child a long time ago, someone who had cut all her ties to her childhood, who was no longer associated with it as an ongoing process.

In the first picture I ever saw of her, a school photograph taken a few months prior, she looked like a prisoner. She had shaved her head, and the hairstyle—or the lack of hairstyle—made her ears protrude and her jaw look sharp, hard.

Helena had a favorite photo of Olga, taken long ago on the rocky beach that they had stopped visiting together. She'd shown it to me several times, proud of having a beautiful child and also, I think, proud of her own accomplishment as a photographer. The photograph was black-and-white, it was handsome, so tasteful that it was hard to believe it showed a real person, a daughter. Olga had long hair. Olga was nude, a bit chubby, a child who seemed slightly too old to not be wearing a swimsuit. A smooth face. She was sitting on the small rocks at the water's edge, squinting slightly at the sun, which I guessed was behind Helena when she took the picture, but she wasn't shading her face with her hands, she hadn't closed her eyes. The squinting made her look angry, adult. She turned to look at the camera as if her name had been called for the picture to be taken; maybe she really was angry in it, because she'd been interrupted in whatever it was she was doing, her playing. The surf was arrested mid-movement, the waves compact, hard and gray. It was the deep blacks in the photograph that had given Olga her adult coloring, which she had when I met her for the first time, those big dark eyebrows, even though I knew from other photographs that she had been a blonde child. She was nothing like herself as a child. I would never have been able to guess that she was the same person.

Helena said that Olga had never liked the rocky beach, she wanted to build sand castles, she wanted to go to the beaches in the tourist villages, by the tavernas hung with fishnets, she wanted to eat ice cream. Helena said she liked the photograph because Olga wasn't prepared for it. It didn't have the self-awareness displayed in other pictures where she was making a funny face or moving her hair with one hand as soon as the camera came out. Now that I'd met Olga I noticed that she still made that same gesture even though she had no hair to push to the side. She was moving a phantom strand, touching her forehead like a religious gesture, compulsively. She did it the first time we met, right after I shook her hand.

ERMOUPOLI WAS CORRODED by sunshine and graffiti; Ermoupoli had colors, had sound, and my fantasies dissolved when they were met with this place, which had kept living in the shadow of its history. From Helena's house the dockyard could be glimpsed like a foothold trap on the shore, huge ships, cranes; the sound of metal filled the air in the daytime, the sound of labor and church bells, the sound of faraway engines.

Helena took me to the square in front of the city hall on my first day, it was a very hot day, she wanted to show it to me, this building I'd already read about, seen pictures of, without telling her. The city hall was yellow with white pilasters and wide steps that led up to three tall doors, beguiling, grand, but worn by time, dilapidated. Helena's heels were cracked in her flapping slides; she had put her hair up. She took me inside, she wanted to show me the ceiling, blue and strewn with stars like the EU flag. An old horse coach was displayed by the entrance, which had hallways on either side, leading to two atria lined by arched walkways and a café, a checkered floor, wooden chairs, stainless steel ashtrays, olive trees. Photographs hung under the arches; they depicted things like rocks, dew on leaves of grass, cinnamon sticks. From a logotype on the bottom of these photographs I gathered that they were part of some sort of campaign initiated by the local government, but it wasn't clear if it was meant for the city's residents or for visitors. They could have been taken anywhere in the world, these photographs; they made me think of expensive technology, expensive editing software, rather than the natural world they portrayed.

Helena's eyes teared up in the sunlight when we came back out; sweat formed on her forehead as we walked toward the harbor, down Chiou, through the markets, the fish, the butchers' clutches of meat. We bought a bottle of water, we bought grapes. I'm glad you're here, I was going crazy, she held the bottle to her temple, to her chest and wrists, she was trying to cool her blood. She told me she was tired of being alone with Olga—was that a horrible thing to say? Oh, not at all. Olga didn't want to do anything, all she wanted was to stay in the house and mope. Olga was glum. She's forgotten what it was like. I love her very much, but. There are times. She paused in front of one of the butchers, then changed her mind and kept moving. I matched her pace, walking slowly in the shade on the main drag. The pavement was slick under my soles, soft from so many other shoes, from rain and sun, the same rain and the same sun but the shoes were different, belonging to people who didn't remember the people who'd walked there long before them, who knew as little about the dead as they did of the as of yet unborn.

The sailboat marina was lined with restaurants; Helena didn't like them. She didn't like the food, she didn't like the patrons. She said: people come here to sunbathe and swim, they know nothing about the culture, the history, nothing about the financial crisis, about the refugees, the world is terrible isn't it, so much pain in the world, but there's nothing to do, we're absolutely powerless, life goes on, c'est la vie as I like to say. She was going to take me to a different spot someday, up by the theater, that place was classy. She'd underestimated the number of late-summer tourists and yearned for the season to end—it's lovely here in fall and spring, so quiet. She had underestimated how warm it was going to be in September— so hot you could melt, don't you think? We walked back along the harbor on a little paved path. There's a museum next to the city hall, she said, in case you want to go one of these days. Three rooms—nothing special. You get tired after a while, so many old things, it feels like eating too much. Helena didn't like bowls, tools, coins. Helena preferred columns, temples, monuments; Helena preferred anything that was great and tall and overwhelming.

I TOOK A PHOTO. I was going to send it to Josef, but I changed my mind: the photo was too beautiful, the photo was an insult. I took it from the balcony off my room, the same vista that Helena had sent when she was trying to convince me to come here. The sea was visible beyond the yellow and pink neighboring houses on the slope leading to the harbor, the antennas in relief against the sky, the phone lines cutting through it. Someone had hung white laundry on the terrace of one of the houses. That's what made the photograph a cliché, I didn't like it, it made me seem silly, oblivious: it should have been colored laundry. I liked the view when I saw it but not after I'd photographed it. I didn't like that the photograph was silent when I was surrounded by sounds: the clanging from the dockyard, the TVs, the birds and the cars.

HELENA'S STREET LOOKED like the Song of Songs, lined with fruits fallen from the trees. In the shade of the walls cats were resting, their eyes gummy, diseased, tongues out, long back legs pretentiously splayed as if they were posing for a photograph. Figs split open in the sun, revealing their red, sticky flesh.

We ate our breakfast in the garden, at the stone table underneath a pergola that Helena had built, or, rather, that she'd had built, many years ago. This garden had shade in the mornings, in between Helena's house and the neighboring house, which was empty, and a low iron fence bordering a small dark alley where nobody ever walked. The fence was older than the building, constructed in the postwar period. It hailed from the city's infancy in the mid-nineteenth century, it wasn't anything complex, an S-shaped pattern; at some point it had been painted pale blue but it had rusted over now, and Helena liked it in that state: it provided a bit of aura, that's the word she used.

The garden's location, the shade and the empty house, made it seem like a secret. We ate yogurt from single-serving containers with honey; flies flocked to the torn foil, attracted by the thin layer that stuck to it. We drank cloudy coffee, Olga drank orange juice from a big glass. No pulp. As time passed the sun found its way through the leaves over the table and Olga left. She was always the first to leave.

On the very first morning we sat down at the table in the seats we would continue to use for the rest of our time there: Helena and Olga with their backs against the house,

me across from them. The first morning I came into the garden from the kitchen and Olga was there alone. I remember
experiencing this as vaguely embarrassing, uncomfortable:
I didn't want to be alone with her; I'd have preferred if she
wasn't there at all. When I sat down I took the chair across
from her since it made the most sense. When Helena joined
us soon thereafter she sat down next to Olga, not me. I didn't
know if they always sat like that, with the mute facade next
door as their view, but it seemed unlikely that they did. In
other words, I'd replaced one of them, I'd taken someone's
spot. I didn't know whose.

THE FRUIT TREES were the pride of Helena's garden. She loved the oranges for their buttery blossoms, the fragrance they produced in spring; it's like paradise to be in the garden at that time of year, she said, to just sit there, in all that beauty, but she didn't enjoy the taste of the fruits—too bitter, too many seeds, she found the peel's dimply texture unpleasant—she picked them to discard or she left them until they fell and rotted on the ground, seafoam-colored maps in the midst of all that yellow. Her pomegranates though, they were tart, sweet, perfect. They hung like heavy lanterns from the thin branches and I loved the twitch when the fruit was picked, the moment it gave, the branch that bounced back. I loved the sound of the peel breaking open, the chambers of the fruit, the membrane, like a heart you could hold in your hand.

In those days, after I'd just arrived in Ermoupoli, a mild atmosphere reigned, a sort of intimacy I'd never known in my own family but which nevertheless felt familiar, the way an infatuation can give you the sense of already having known someone you only recently learned existed and therefore could not possibly have missed. In the morning, when I walked down the spiral staircase that linked the top floor to the kitchen, I had the feeling of having walked those steps many times before. Helena, repeating: I want you to feel free here, this is a place where you can be yourself, I don't want you to feel like you need to be a certain way—she was addressing both me and Olga, as if we were both her daughters.

Helena and Olga lived very close and also very far from each other.

Olga often walked off. Olga ate fast. Olga sat in the garden and drew in a big sketch pad, she had lots of different pencils, the graphite varying degrees of softness; Helena was eager to see what she was drawing; sometimes she wasn't allowed. When Olga did show her work—to Helena only, fastidiously turned away from me so I wouldn't catch a glimpse—Helena invariably said, this is really quite good, very good, what a talent!, in a tone I felt was sarcastic. I recognized that tone; it scared me when she used it on me but when I heard her use it on Olga it had the opposite effect: it made me feel at ease. It made me feel valuable. During these days Helena was warm toward me, more so than ever, chatty, laughed a lot; she said: you're a funny one, aren't you, she moaned loudly when she ate the food I cooked for dinner, what flavors. She kept repeating how happy she was I was there, that it was good, so fun, and her insistence moved me. I was greedy for her love. I knew she didn't give it easily.

She took me to the rocky beach. A bus to the other side of the island followed by a narrow trail down a steep hill you had to walk by foot—this meant, she said, that not a lot of people came there, she liked to swim naked, stretch out in the gravel. Nature was dry and colorless around us as we walked. The sea roared down below, blue and furiously foaming, hard at the edges. Helena swam like she was fighting the waves, flinging herself at them with great force. Her large breasts hung like they were droopy dough when she came out of the water. A wide scar slashed above her sex and I looked

34

away so as not to embarrass her or myself. I was not naked. I closed my eyes against the light and listened to the break hitting the beach like breaths. Helena's voice, a little sluggish: this is the life. Her Stockholm accent creaked through the words, a dialect belonging to a generation distinct from mine; I loved it, so comforting, the sound of old TV shows. Her breasts spread when she lay down on her towel and she hummed to herself as if trying to chase away some thought. This is the life; I was warm from the sun and from the love I imagined was radiating from her and from me, between us. I thought: here she is with a friend, here she is with a person she holds dear, someone who understands her, perhaps better than anybody else.

I barely interacted with Olga during these days. She was quiet. She was shy. She was not at all the way I'd imagined her. When I saw her, when I let my gaze linger for too long by mistake, I often felt embarrassed by the picture I'd previously construed of her. I worried that these old thoughts were seeping out and gave her the upper hand. I was a bit scared of her and I was still jealous, a feeling that made me feel ugly, big, clumsy.

We ate pomegranates all the time; we picked the trees clean. Antioxidants, Helena said, food for a long life. The juice got in under my short nails when I peeled the fruits and the color stained my skin, thin bright lines; they burned when I swam in the sea, wide strokes in the salty water that got in everywhere. Olga liked to grab a handful of seeds from the bowl as I was peeling the fruit, her arm grazing mine; she would come from behind, quick as lightning, she'd toss them into her open mouth like a monkey and then go out into the garden where she'd sit down, where I could see her without her seeing me inside the kitchen. Her jaws working, the crackling, the juice. As I followed the contours of Olga's face my hands were red.

2.

Atlas

IT WAS NOVEMBER WHEN I MET HELENA the first time. I got to her house in the afternoon and a mere hour later it was pitch-black outside. The darkness made it seem as if we'd been sitting there for a long time, deep in conversation.

That time I assumed that she and Olga had lived in their apartment for many years, a lifetime, but I came to learn that they had only just moved back to Sweden, that they hadn't been in Stockholm for more than a year, and I realized that the feeling of belonging I'd sensed in the apartment—not coziness exactly, but specifically a sense of belonging—was not the result of yearslong habits but rather Helena's apparently innate ability to take possession of every place she set foot.

The apartment smelled of toast and garlic. Helena's perfume was in the coats and scarves in the hall, like she'd been marking her territory.

They'd moved from London around Christmas. Olga had done a spring semester at a school in the city, within walking distance from the apartment, but it didn't "work," a word Helena pronounced with scare quotes and no further explanation. Then, in the fall, she'd started another new school, a boarding school, a concept I thought sounded cruel and anachronistic. They'd chosen it because of its international profile. That didn't "work" either. Helena said: my daughter doesn't like school. She'd thought boarding school would suit Olga better; there were students speaking all kinds of languages there, students from all over the world, but it was no use, something to do with the school's culture, issues with the other students, girls who'd cover their stalls with towels when they showered, all that intimacy was too much, living with your classmates.

As Helena was speaking I pictured the book about Thérèse and Isabelle. I pictured a very old school: dormitories, wrought-iron beds, brick buildings, a place that looked more like my idea of an old sanatorium or prison than any of the schools I had attended.

Olga made no friends. Olga became depressed. Olga developed strange phobias, for instance a fear of biking, she was scared of skidding and dying on the rural gravel roads north of Stockholm. You couldn't get ahold of her anymore. She didn't pick up her phone. Helena called her several times a day, and every time Olga didn't respond Helena thought she was dead, she called and she called and was consumed by fear that transformed first into anger and then relief once Olga finally responded—always by text, never with a call, and Helena loathed texting. But at least she was in a safe place. Better than in the city, where there were too many things that could happen, too many people; Helena no longer trusted Olga, everything was different now that she was getting older, in the past Olga was always following her around like a shadow, she was so sweet. A school photo was stuck to the fridge, the first picture I saw of her, the school uniform, her shorn head; Helena told me about the hair she'd shaved off, she couldn't let go, Olga's long hair, her thick hair, Helena said: the kind of hair anyone would dream of, but she didn't want it, you know how it is, some fast while others starve.

I didn't like Olga then. I felt like she was putting on airs.

You've got to give it time, Helena said, she's used to more bohemian environments, and I felt a quiver of hate run over my skin. I thought I could become Helena's daughter, Olga's proxy, a better version of her, one much more worthy of love.

But that was later. The first time I met Helena I knew very little about her life. I was there to do an interview.

THE FIRST TIME I met Helena I spent a long time walking around trying to find her address before I located the correct door; it was a green building in the Atlas neighborhood, French balconies with columns, meanders in the stairwell, a swastika crowning the elevator cage. I climbed the stairs to her floor. It was the week after two big terrorist attacks and I was irrationally tense and dealt with it by never letting myself rest, constantly moving my eyes, registering and naming everything I saw, a small child, a dog, a bus, a tree, a 7-Eleven. I did not want to ride the elevator.

For weeks afterward the elevator was out of service for repairs. Inside the cage the shaft was empty and naked. I took the stairs again. Everything I'd noticed the first time, the meanders, the curved railing that ended and then began again on either side of the large windows, the children's shoes on the doormat on the second floor, the red lamp button on floor three that I had to locate in the murk since by that point the timed light had turned off, it all became familiar and imprinted on my memory so that I soon stopped registering anything. Not the shoes, not the meanders. I no longer read the names on the doors; when I reached her floor, I knew without looking which one was Helena's.

I had the thought that I'd known already the first time I walked those stairs that it wouldn't be the last time, that it wasn't fear that made me note every detail but certainty. I imagined that I had seen the future the first time I was at Helena's and that what I'd seen walking up the stairs wasn't what was in front of me but rather an image from my own memory.

AFTER OUR CONVERSATION I had to listen to the recording over and over again. The sound was bad, my phone had captured some kind of noise, a whirring, maybe from her computer or mine, the fridge, the pipes. I had to rewind again and again to hear what she was saying, to catch her phrasing. I did not skip the silent stretches that nobody but me would have been able to interpret but which I knew were the sounds of Helena pulling up photos of her paintings on her computer or phone. I pictured her hands while I listened to these fuzzy silences. She clicked hard, as if the movement of her hand and not the touch was what conjured a new image. Her hands were tanned and veiny, a grid of age and work stretched over slender knuckles, she zoomed and made the pictures grainy, she used her fingers to indicate on the wall in front of us, I want to give you a sense of the dimensions. While listening I pictured the early Christmas lights in the windows across the yard. The disorder in her apartment, a large painted porcelain bowl with opened government mail and invoices, pens, keys, a bank fob; her big weeping fig with yellow leaves. Her voice on my recording: this is my house in Greece. She was showing me a photo I'd later understand had been taken from the balcony of what came to be my bedroom in Ermoupoli. An incredible, hazy light, the light of dusk. It really was a lovely photo, one I produced out of the darkroom of my mind again and again as I listened to the recording, my house in Greece, a beat of silence. I love Greece, she said in a way that filled me with discomfort. I wanted to correct her but didn't know for what.

She showed me an installation view from another show a couple of years prior, the gallery in Berlin, she asked me if I'd been; the building straddled the border between East and West, what an amazing building, so full of history, she loved the mosaics in the stairwell there, she loved the Turkish market by the canal, the plastic-bagged halka tatlisi she used to buy for her daughter when she was little. Did I know she'd lived there, no, I didn't know; I should've said yes since it was on her website. It was where she met her ex-husband, she said, her daughter's father, though she didn't think highly of him, I mean this was ancient history, she said, a few years around the turn of the millennium, right before the year 2000, I mean that's almost twenty years ago at this point, God.

This interview, one of several in a series I'd been contracted to do for a fashion magazine that fall, was to be written as if the interviewee were speaking freely, as if the text were a transcript. In reality the texts were, of course, a hybrid of sorts, a fantasy about how these women—a playwright, a jewelry designer, a cinematographer, and an artist, Helena, the oldest of the four, and as far as I could tell cast precisely in the role of older woman—would have spoken if their speech were beautiful and coherent. The interview would be accompanied by a portrait, the main feature of the spread, and Helena confided in me that she was anxious about the shoot. She didn't like seeing herself in photos. She was always self-conscious of the situation as such, the photographer had all the power, she felt vulnerable, didn't know what to do with her hands, didn't know how to control her face, she disliked the way her lips revealed her gums when she smiled—she showed me, a grinning, joyless smile that made her look like she was about to attack—I said: I'm the same way, I don't like being photographed either, even though that was a lie, I didn't feel strongly one way or another.

I'd always found it difficult to resist the illusion of intimacy created by interviews. I liked the fixed roles. I liked being the inquisitive party, enjoyed being able to ask almost anything of someone who had up until very recently been a stranger. I often confused the confidences made in these settings with true intimacy, as if there were real closeness between us and not just me closing in on the other. I felt excited when I left Helena's apartment; I started fantasizing about future conversations with her before I'd even made it home, conversations where our roles were switched and she asked me questions too, listening intently.

AFTERWARD I SPENT so much time with the sound of her voice, her silences, my own fantasies, that it soon felt like we were close friends. I thought it would be easy to portray her, that she'd be very flattered by my text. She had asked to read it before I filed. I emailed her, expecting praise in return. She hated it. Another email came the second after I'd read the first, and this time she wrote: Forgive me, I let my emotions get the best of me, it's just that I don't recognize my own voice. It won't do. You'll have to do it over. Get in touch pronto. Best H.

I froze. I was devastated and furious. I felt as though I'd been rejected by a lover. "Pronto" made me feel panicked; I didn't understand if it was wrath or humor. My strong feelings surprised me: they meant something.

I listened to the recording of our conversation once again, this time looking for evidence. I was right. She really had said the things I had written. It was herself she hated, not me. I noted this for my own sake. I understood that I'd heard something I wasn't meant to hear, that I'd gotten her to say something unflattering—though it was impossible for me to understand what, because nothing she'd said was particularly remarkable. She talked about her work. She talked about her long days, which began in the morning and often continued into the wee hours of the night. She talked about the importance of freedom and alone time and rest. She talked about her back and her hallux valgus, which sometimes made it hard for her to stand for long—that part I hadn't included in the piece. She talked about Maria Lassnig, whom she admired, those pinks and greens. After the conversation I'd gone hunting like a crazy person for a painting by Dorothea Tanning that had put Helena in a trance when she saw it at the Miró Foundation in Barcelona, but I never found it and could only imagine what it looked like, the power it had wielded over her. I was jealous of her accounts of strong experiences of beauty. She said predictable things like "it went straight to the heart," "it was as if time had stopped." She didn't seem scared of sounding banal or uncritical.

But she was scared. She was vain. I sensed an aching tenderness sprouting in me. I didn't want her to be mad at me. I wanted her to let me understand her.

We agreed to a second interview. My fee was not in proportion to the work but I couldn't bear the thought of her dissatisfaction, the prospect of her thinking me an idiot who had made her sound like someone she wasn't. I wanted to win the approval I'd taken out ahead of time and then lost. We decided I'd visit her studio on the outskirts of the city. This time it was dark outside already when I left the house, it was an unusually mild fall, we were approaching First Advent Sunday.

SHE WAS PLAYING Étienne Daho from her computer. La notte, la notte. I didn't ask; she told me, I love this record. The sound was muted, metallic, and the studio was lit by white lamps, a smell of soap and limestone. She had made coffee. She seemed to have dressed up in a way I couldn't quite define since my recollection of her outfit the first time was muddled by the many times I'd pictured her since then. She was more beautiful than I remembered, or different. This is much better, she told me, this is me in my element, it was too weird at home, I think that's where things went wrong, I'm sensitive to energies, this is a more professional setting.

She cleared her throat and unfolded a piece of paper she'd kept in her shirt pocket. Have some coffee! I served us both. Milk? Thanks, I'm fine. She'd put out a full carton. The music was rattling from the laptop and it would have been better to turn it off for the recording, but I also wanted to please her. Saxophone, a whispering female voice.

This is what I want you to write, she said, and she held the paper up in front of her. A printout, double-sided. She began reading, and then she paused. Are you recording? Maybe you could just give me the text, I said, or email it to me. Yes, she said, but I want us to do it the right way this time, so we get it right.

She kept reading. She held the paper in front of her, arms stretched out.

The text was complete nonsense. It had none of the emotion and honesty of the first interview. Her sentences were complicated and pompous. I listened, despondent. It made me embarrassed, even as the self-image that she was now revealing to me increased my tenderness. She seemed uncomfortable; her reading was stilted and a bit too fast so that she stumbled on the particularly clunky sentences. Once finished she asked: Do you have any questions?

I tried to make it seem like I was pondering what she'd shared. This is good, I said. It might be a bit too long. She rummaged in her shirt pocket and found a pencil stub, placed the paper on the table between us, and struck out a couple of lines. Something like that, maybe? But you're the expert, she said, I'm sure you can clean it up, I trust you. She gave me the printout. A compact transcript, entirely without line breaks.

I feel it's important that we do this well, she said. I'm sure you feel the same way. I care a lot about quality, I'm pedantic about it. Me too, I said. I'm glad you're so thorough, it's important that we get it right, you've given me a lot of material to work with. I conferred with myself about how I could cut her text in half. Your interview was one of the best I've done in a long while, I said, I really enjoyed talking to you. This was true. Nevertheless, I was embarrassed by the way I flattered her, my ill-concealed motives, my desire for her to like me. Oh, she exclaimed, did you really. She said it in an especially condescending way, not directed at me but sort of inward, as if she was mocking herself. I'm sorry I'm so fucking annoying, she said, but it's just the way I am, I felt it was important, to get it right. I agreed with her, yes, yes, no, no. Everything she thought was important I thought was important too.

WE EMAILED back and forth a couple of times. My emails were polite, hers more straightforward and at the same time wilder; she frequently fired off several in close sequence. She started signing off with "xx," which I found a bit embarrassing, casual in an affected way, although it flattered me that she was trying to seem casual in front of me. I heard myself describing her to Josef and Alain as if she were a joke, and it was satisfying and mean, it was a spell against my own need for affirmation, it disarmed her, it satisfied my need to talk and think about her, to analyze her behavior and her word choices. Josef thought she seemed like an idiot. Alain said, in English: she sounds crazy. It hurt my feelings that they agreed with me when I talked about her like this. It pleased me too. It made me feel like I was good at reading people, like I could see past appearances.

Christmas came and went and almost every day was as dark as night; neon icicles hung from the trees and Kungsträdgården was suffused with an aroma of warm sugar from the café huts. Kids and teens skated on the rink to a soundtrack of love songs, and it made me both anxious and happy to walk through the park where the city opened up like a carnival or a harbor with its red and green lights, the noise from the cars and the fast-food chains on both sides of the street.

Every time I checked my email I longed and hoped for a message from her. I wanted to find a way to extend our exchange. I couldn't explain why, neither to myself nor anybody else. I wasn't sure if she liked me; I really wanted her to like me.

When the interview with its portrait was out I wrote to ask how she felt about it. Instead of answering she responded and asked if she could call, she proposed a time, I felt nervous and expectant. Leading up to the agreed-upon time I was at home, waiting in silence. One minute after she was supposed to call I got a call from an unknown number, not the one I'd saved as hers, but I answered anyway after a few ringtones. A male voice on the line: hi my name is—, I'm calling from—, I interrupted him, incoherent, I'm expecting a call, I can't talk, I hung up. Later I searched the number: probably a scam. The minutes passed and I cursed the stranger who might have sabotaged my chance to—what? I couldn't say.

She called me half an hour later. She said she hated the photo, awful, she couldn't even look at it, she hadn't been able to compel the photographer to do it over, and in contrast this put me in a good light because she loved the interview. She told me she felt I'd captured her perfectly. I'd made very few adjustments to the text she'd given me, basically just shortened it and translated it into English. She went on and on about it, how happy it had made her to read it, to recognize the words that were her own but also not, it was like seeing herself from the outside. This text made her interested in herself; it was almost like falling in love. It's wonderful, she said, to meet someone who's made such an effort to understand you.

It was only with the enormous relief I felt when she told me this that I understood how scared I'd been that she'd be mad at me, how much I wanted to hear something like "you've captured me." I didn't care that it was her own words, not mine, that had brought about that feeling; I was happy to be her mirror. The praise she piled onto her own writing made me cringe, but it also gave me a sense of power, a heady combination.

I agreed, yes it is wonderful. I asked where she was right now. In the studio, but she was about to leave. I told her I was in the neighborhood; I wasn't. Would she want to see me? I told her I wanted to keep talking, that we'd only scratched the surface. There's so much I'd like to ask you.

After a short silence, which I interpreted as hesitation but which could just as well have been her pretending to hesitate, she said, yes, I'd be happy to. She was, I soon realized, as lonely as I was.

THAT WINTER I'D LOST a hard drive containing thousands of photos. I didn't remember exactly what they depicted, I hadn't looked at those pictures in many years, all I knew was that they were all from a certain period, several years of my life that I no longer felt particularly connected to; still, it had been a comfort to know that those photos existed, that they were within reach on a black hard drive that had now disappeared, perhaps in the trash, perhaps into the hands of someone for whom these photos had no meaning whatsoever and who would replace them with their own photos.

I knew that there were photos of other people on this hard drive, people who had once meant a lot to me and with whom I was no longer in contact. After losing the pictures I suddenly wanted to reach out to apologize for having robbed them of these memories they didn't know they had. I didn't.

So far each of my romantic relationships had left me lonelier than I was before, in a way I didn't quite understand. Every breakup robbed me of a social world I thought I was naturally part of. I lost friends. I fell in and out of love easily, and I often exited relationships in ways that people around me, the people I'd thought were close friends who understood me, seemed to view as amoral, almost illegal, and this made me feel even more lonely, fundamentally lonely, a loneliness I was never free from. I heard things about myself through the grapevine: you can't trust her.

But I never did anything wrong. I was just looking for love. I was looking for someone who could reflect me back to myself. I was looking for someone who could bring me into their world. I wanted to obliterate myself, be emptied and filled, but I never found what I was looking for. I was never as interested in the other person as I was in the person I became in their eyes. And when I'd stopped being someone in their eyes, or when I no longer wanted to be the person I was to them, there was nothing left. No tenderness. I had to find someone else immediately, something new, a new version of myself. I was waiting for something calamitous, something that would change everything.

During the period of my life whose evidence I had now lost with the hard drive, I'd been in a romantic relationship, the longest I'd ever had and in many ways the most important one, the one that time revolved around. There was a before and an after. I was young when we met and felt old by the time our relationship ended.

There was one picture among the lost photos—at least, it was a picture I never found anywhere else so I assumed it had been on the hard drive—that I remembered very clearly. Or rather, I remembered the moment I'd taken it. The picture helped me remember, even though it didn't tell a grand story. We were by the sea on Sweden's west coast, pretending to be a dogged old couple despite not knowing each other very well yet; at that point in our relationship I had no patience, I wanted immediately, as soon as possible, to get to the point where it would feel as if we'd known each other forever, as if the boundaries between us were blurry, ideally erased altogether, so that it would be impossible to picture her without picturing me at the same time. We were picking objects from the beach, shards of glass, oyster shells birds had flung at the rocks; I kept them stacked in my hand even though

I had no use for them and wasn't planning to keep them. I can still remember the sensation of the shells in my hand, the space between thumb and index finger that grew as the stack grew, the rough coating on the shells, hard plates that made them look like polypores, the smooth insides, mother-of-pearl white, expensive. I remember that the sky was white and that it made all the other colors seem brighter, the rock face pink, the sea green, but in the photo I took that day, the photo I never found again, everything looked gray.

I didn't mourn the life we'd had together. I didn't mourn our romance. I didn't miss her in a painful way. But I did miss my faith that this love story would be forever, that the life we were living together would go on forever, and I missed my conviction that if either of us ever left the other she would be associated with great pain. I had looked forward to having a sad memory. Sometimes when I passed the building where we'd lived, in an apartment whose windows weren't visible from the street, I remembered the melancholia I used to conjure when I walked home on dark days with light coming from the windows—not ours—and I pictured how at some point in the future, when this building would no longer be part of my daily life, I would walk this same street and re-member a world I'd lost. But the melancholia I felt then was dependent on my still loving her, and I no longer loved her, and I felt nothing when I passed this building now.

I'd heard about an ancient custom, damnatio memoriae, condemnation of memory, the practice of destroying picto-rial and textual records in order to eliminate a person from history. The loss of my photographs reminded me of this custom. I'd seen paintings where one face among the others had been erased, frescoes in muddy colors, family portraits with four bodies but just three faces. The viewer's gaze was immediately drawn to the dark space where the obliterated face used to be. While the surrounding faces, the preserved faces with their large eyes and small mouths seemed like they could belong to anybody, someone who had never existed, that darkness had a trace of a real person. That empty space told me: this used to be someone who no longer exists. It brought to mind old family portraits where dead children were photographed along with the living and where they, because of the camera's long shutter speed, often appeared clearer, more alive, than their siblings and parents who were ghostlike and blurry in the frozen, extended moment of the photograph.

I would have liked to see my lost photographs. They held no interest to me until they became impossible to find. At the same time, the loss made me feel free. There was no longer any evidence of this period in my life. Now I could create my own narrative about it; now I could create a new life for myself.

SOON I WAS SEEING Helena several times a week. I made myself available whenever she called. I canceled plans I'd made with others in order to see her. I isolated myself to be available to her, but I never felt lonely. I didn't feel isolated. I felt that my life held a meaning that had been missing for a long time.

Helena could not stand routines other than the ones she made for herself, the contours of work and recovery; she liked to get in touch at short notice and then she liked to change the time of our meetup at even shorter notice. At seven she might call because she wanted to meet at a restaurant for dinner at eight, and twenty minutes later she'd call again to propose: how about seven thirty, I'm already around the corner, when can you be here?

This made it hard to say no to her since it always felt like we were in a rush, like every time might be the last time. I constantly had the sense of being on the precipice of a big mistake, something that might change our relationship, destroy it. I never wanted to say no when she called me. Sometimes days went by without a word from her and those days I was sad, abandoned, desperate, and I couldn't tell anyone how I was feeling.

I met up with Josef in the orchestra bar. I talked about Helena. I talked about her blood sugar crashes and her mood swings; I made fun of her. I talked about her in this way in order to keep her to myself: I didn't want him to be curious about meeting her, didn't want him to take her from me.

I hated her a little on the days she didn't get in touch

with me; my view of her was from a remove: she was self-obsessed, moody, vain. It was easy to have these thoughts when I wasn't seeing her. Several times I resolved not to answer the next time she got in touch. I wasn't going to see her again, she didn't make me feel good, it was an unhealthy, one-sided relationship, she was toxic to me, she was mean, she was weird. But I also loved her on these days, I loved her more than before, even from that distance: her bad traits made her infinitely more fascinating, made her approval even more precious, I couldn't understand why she hated me, why she didn't call. But she always called again, and I always went to see her, and the thoughts and feelings I'd had in her absence faded. She made me feel important and meaningful. With her I felt that there was a social context I wouldn't lose this time, that wouldn't expel me—she and I, we were enough together, we didn't need anybody else. I had never met someone like her before. I liked the fact that she was older than me. I liked her rough edges and her seriousness. I stopped talking about her with Josef and Alain because I didn't like it when they repeated the bad things I had said about her. It hurt me as if someone had badmouthed a family member of mine. I was allowed to do it, nobody else.

I started spending afternoons and some evenings in her atelier while she worked. She had an assistant she didn't like, another artist, younger. She thought he was sloppy, shy, solipsistic. Since I never got to meet him it was easy for me to agree on all his shortcomings. I agreed with her in order to make her like me more, to amplify the contrast between him and me. I helped her with stuff, whatever she asked for, little things. I made her coffee, bought her smokes, wrote her emails, which she dictated and signed with "H." For the first time since we met she asked me more questions than I asked her, though she continued talking about herself.

She requested my presence. She wanted my opinion on a particular color. She wanted to know if she should cut her hair or if it would make her look old. Her hair was wavy, big but porous, sort of airy. She wanted to know if it was still thick enough. When she was my age it had been curly like a painting of Lilith, she showed me photos, she used a lot of eyeliner back then. It made her look old when she was still young. She used to be a little chubby, her face was round in the old pictures, age had come with stronger contours. She didn't look like herself. She was more beautiful now. But I still missed the young version of her and I wished we could have met, I wondered if we'd have liked each other, the thought that she might not have liked me if we'd been the same age made me angry and sad. Our age difference appeared a prerequisite for our relationship: the fact that I was young, different, uninformed about certain things that came with experience.

I made us dinner in the studio. Bachelor food you could cook on the hot plate in the kitchenette, fish sticks, mac and cheese, frozen pyttipanna with fried eggs. Sometimes, on days when her pain was flaring, she wanted to eat in Atlas. She'd soak her achy joints in the tub while I relished the knives in the kitchen, the materials, the four plates of the stove, the darkness and the light and the smells of this apartment, this home that wasn't mine. I always wished she'd invite me to sleep there because I often stayed late on these nights, long into the night, but it never happened. I returned to my own apartment, which was dark and empty and silent, smelling of nothing.

There were long stretches while she worked in the studio when I had nothing to do. I'd sit down and flip through her books. I loved a book of photographs by Herbert List, taken in Greece in the 1930s, crumbling columns and men who resembled statues. It astonished me that the photos were so old. They looked like perfume campaigns from the eighties. They reminded me of a scene from *If . . .* , a film I'd been mesmerized by when I saw it on TV as a teenager, a scene showing a man practicing gymnastics, heaving himself up by the arm and then flipping around a tall bar as a younger boy observed him. Memories of this scene had stayed with me for a long time, a close-up of the man from behind, the viewer saw him put chalk on his hands and clap them together, saw the muscles playing over his back as he got into position, saw the pores of his hands, dark over gray scale.

After the film was shown on TV I had no way of seeing those frames again, this one scene that had stuck with me. Much later it turned out that Alain had had a similar experience of that same film, at the same age as me, and of precisely that same scene, which he too claimed to remember in exact detail. It was a rare bright spot in our otherwise pretty strained relationship, a beautiful notion that the two of us, each on our own continent and long before we met, long before we could even have imagined each other, had shared the same obscure fascination and desire while watching this scene. The joy of the discovery didn't last long, however, because his recollection was completely different from mine. He asserted that the man's face had been in the shot, and that it had been the chest muscles playing, not the back.

We downloaded the movie to resolve our disagreement. At least that's how I thought of it even though we both danced around the subject, we should watch it to check if it's still good, we should show Josef, show him this part of our shared history, perhaps our only shared history. Alain had wanted to make movies for a while, film was his first love, the original, unrequited love, and normally I hated watching movies with him. He showed me *Pink Narcissus*. He showed me the work of Kenneth Anger. He wouldn't stop talking. He wanted to explain everything. Josef saw what was going on and thought we were being ridiculous. He fell asleep long before we'd gotten to the scene Alain and I were anticipating with gritted teeth.

It turned out that reality was nothing like my memory, but it also wasn't like Alain's. The scene was filmed from a distance. The man was dressed and you could see neither his back nor his chest, not his hands up close, not his face. It was, I realized, as if the boy's besotted gaze had been transposed onto us. We agreed that it wasn't as good as we'd remembered it, and we never spoke about it again.

I rarely saw Josef anymore, not Alain either.

THAT SPRING HELENA talked a lot about her house in Ermoupoli. She wasn't able to go right then, and she didn't
know when she'd be able to. She mourned the orange-tree
blossoms she'd miss, it's paradise, paradise, she said this
word again and again.

Helena also talked about her daughter a lot, her problems
in school, Olga didn't want to do anything, she just wanted
to read, be alone. I came to associate these two things, Olga
and Ermoupoli, two parts of Helena's life that remained hidden to me, that I didn't have access to, making me jealous
and mean. I wanted her to invite me to the house. The two
of us, alone. I wanted to have her house. I wanted to be her
daughter.

Helena told me the story of seeing the city for the first
time in the 1990s, she was my age, she'd been given an
artist stipend and had divorced her first husband, so she
went on what she termed her reverse honeymoon, she went
island-hopping in Greece, something she'd never done before though both of her sisters had done it when they were
young, and back then Helena had thought they were silly,
she'd wanted to distance herself from everything everyone
else her age was doing when she was young, but now all she
wanted was to sprawl out on the volcanic sand and let herself be swallowed by the sea, which was even bluer in real life
than it was in the travel catalogs. She went to Mykonos and
to Delos, where she photographed the ruins, just like Herbert
List. She went to Ermoupoli to change ferries, it was pure
chance. She said: I couldn't believe my eyes, it was like time

travel, it was like nothing else, streets of marble, the neoclassical palaces eroding in the harsh sun, in the hard, salty water. She stayed for several weeks. She'd dreamed of returning there ever since and made her dream come true years later, when she had Olga.

Helena had enjoyed being pregnant, the care extended by strangers, the attention. I had the sense that she was pleased I didn't have any kids of my own: it made me available to her, and it gave her an existential upper hand.

It made me bitter to hear her talk about Ermoupoli. I didn't like to be reminded of her life without me, a life where she hadn't needed me. I lay awake at night and thought about her daughter, fantasized about her, made caricatures of her, evil images, blurry images. I didn't actually know what she looked like; I had only seen a few photos. I made her ugly. The city, on the other hand, was amazingly beautiful in my imagination, painfully beautiful. I longed for it. I longed to be welcome in a place that was beautiful.

HELENA'S DAD was waiting to die. His deteriorating health had been one of the reasons for her return to Sweden, which meant that his death was a precondition of our friendship.

This man, a man she'd been afraid of as a child, his loud voice and flaring temper, traits she ended up inheriting, this man who she'd already mourned for many years though he was still alive, the intimacy they had lost, the respect she had lost for him after he lost the power to scare or validate her, after his authority lost its meaning when he was replaced by other authorities in her life, other men, other institutions— this man now broke up the rhythm of my life with his impending death, which made Helena stop working because he had become her work, being with him, being with her mother and sisters. It was a matter of weeks. Weeks became a month, became one and a half. We don't give up so easily in our family, she said, it's in our blood, that appetite for life.

Up until then she'd always talked about herself as if her life had begun in her twenties, which was when she had grown into herself. Now she told me about her childhood. She talked about how much she had admired her father as a child; she used the word "immensely." She said: I'd have liked to be a dad myself, there's something special about a father figure. She had loved listening to his stories about the world. She envied the ability of men to explain what it was all about, an ability she'd tried to conquer all her life.

She wanted to see me whenever possible; we saw each other in her parents' neighborhood, she wanted to look at objects at the Auction Works, buy a bag of Jamaican coffee at Sibyllan, she wanted to go shopping, she needed more life, she had to drink a glass of champagne. He's old, she said, it's life, it is what it is, that's the way life goes, c'est la vie; she babbled maniacally about her dad, he's lived his life, he's over ninety years old, she told me he was ill-tempered, unsentimental in the face of death. Anger tends to be a secondary emotion, it can hide grief. Helena told me that her mom grew kinder with every year. I didn't like to hear her say "Mom" and "Dad," the words capitalized, it sounded babyish and coddled, creepy and embarrassing. I didn't like to think that she had parents. These links that tethered Helena to the world had appeared out of nowhere, when she'd previously seemed completely unfettered.

She seemed to share this unease, she told me she didn't feel comfortable at her parents', they'd moved to this apartment when she was already well into adulthood, a home where they'd already been old for more than a quarter century. The interiors were old-fashioned; the smells, the food they ate, Swedish and anodyne. The family heirlooms, which had been dispersed throughout the large apartment of her childhood, had been stuffed into this smaller space, furniture made a century ago lined up like objects in a museum; it was cramped and stagnant, nothing matched, it was depressing to her to see these clumsy, expensive pieces in a home without thresholds.

She didn't like her sisters. For years they'd talked about getting together at the family's summer house, a house Helena described as "grotesque," ostentatious, way too large; they talked about clearing it out, they had to get started, it was high time, they talked about a "sibling weekend" as if that were some kind of hallowed tradition, but Helena had never been part of any adult sisterhood since leaving Sweden and now she felt excluded. The others had inside jokes Helena didn't understand, they had memories she wasn't part of; this comforted me—their distance made me feel closer to her.

Helena's sisters were both younger than her and closer to each other in age. The older of the two was a widow and after her husband died it was as if she were the oldest of the group, Helena told me. She has such mom vibes, she was always the one you had to feel sorry for, she was the one who kept her chin up; Helena told me it was so typical of her sister to become a widow, you know what I mean? She seemed to view it as a character flaw that her brother-in-law had not reached advanced age the way her flesh-and-blood relatives had. The kids were too young when it happened, she told me, too young to understand anything, it's just so sad to be honest. Helena explained that there was something wrong with these kids, her nieces. They were twenty-something but seemed like teenagers, like twelve-year-olds. They had bad skin, obviously they can't help it, but she couldn't . . . , she just felt like . . . , no, she had to say it: their untreated acne, their greasy hair, it seemed like a sign of some sort of love deficit, her sister was very, she paused, searching for the right word—cold, that's what she is, she said, sounding as if she'd held on to this assessment for a long time without having anyone to share it with, she's cold, you can't deny it. Not a good mother to the nieces. They were quiet and shy and morose. They had childish interests. Fantasy books, they went to fairs and conventions, they played dress-up, collected little toys, they were in med school but they were scared of blood. Helena felt they'd been too controlled; she believed that their disrupted childhood was now leaking into their dead-serious adult games, there was something sick about it, like Michael Jackson's Neverland. They didn't like Olga, she knew this with certainty; they thought she took up either too much space or too little, their mom must have done something or said something to make them dislike her, she just knew it, Olga is a trailblazer, she said, Olga doesn't follow other people's opinions, they thought Helena had failed as a parent, that she was a bad mother, a bad person, they can't handle someone being independent and free.

I often got confused when Helena talked about her family. She lumped together her nieces the way she lumped together her own sisters, twosomes she was excluded from. The only account she ever gave of her youngest sister was that she came across as cowed, needy, she was the middle sister's henchman, always agreed with her, never stated her own opinion, never thought for herself; Helena told me: it doesn't feel like we're part of the same family, obviously that's a terrible thing to say, but she just couldn't understand how they turned out like that, so negative, so prim, we always had big parties growing up, tons of people, wonderful Christmas celebrations, those holidays were heavenly, the food and the tree that reached all the way to the ceiling, it was wonderful to go to cut down the tree with Dad, the freezing cold and the lake, all the candles and the presents later on. She missed those Christmases so much it hurt, she had never been able to re-create anything like them, they were never the same again. She had zero desire to go to the summer house. It was where she'd had her happy childhood, where she'd eaten cherries from the tree and spat the pits in a ring around the trunk, where they made a wall of jam, you had to time it right, get the cherries just when they ripened, before the birds got to them. That's where she'd jumped from the dock, where she'd eaten filmjölk with crispbread and smoked fish, where she and her sisters had played hide-and-seek in the enormous, grotesque house where you could get lost if you wanted to and unless you knew every nook and cranny from hundreds of thousands of hours playing that very game. That's where they'd played Monopoly with tin tokens, I always picked the hat, she said, and she always lost because she focused on buying the streets with the prettiest names, she didn't build anything, just collected street upon street until she ran out of money, had no strategy other than her desire for beauty. That's where she'd read *Asterix and Cleopatra*, there was a meal she'd never been able to forget in that comic book: pearls dissolved in vinegar, can you imagine. That's where she'd had secrets, that's where she'd gone through puberty, that's where she'd been angry. She had no desire to go. She had no desire to stay in Sweden. Why didn't her sisters go to the house themselves if they wanted to go there so badly, if they loved it so much, if they were so eager to dig into what used to be, wallow in the past. Not her! She lived for the future.

Helena's dad was mean to her, he made painful jokes about his death. Gallows humor is so lonely, she said, why does he have to make a joke of it.

IT DIDN'T SURPRISE ME that Helena was born rich. Something about her way of taking command of other people, her flippant and sometimes disrespectful attitude to luxury paired with how casually she surrounded herself with things that were not luxurious—cheap synthetic materials, big-pack discount groceries, two-in-one hair care—had led me to suspect as much. I found a certain pleasure in fantasizing about her family, her evil widowed sister, who, Helena had told me as if to balance it out, was very beautiful. I'd have liked to see a photograph of her. I would have liked to see photos of all of Helena's family, her summer holidays, her Christmases; I would have liked to see photos of her as a child, and one time I asked because she'd already shown me lots of photos of herself in London and Berlin, photos of her daughter as a child, so I thought it wouldn't be out of line to ask; she told me she didn't have any such photographs.

I made my own pictures instead, of the sister in particular, a picture that recurred so often that I could barely remember that I'd never met this woman, that this woman, the one I pictured in my head, did not exist. I imagined her hair. I imagined a strong jaw; I imagined her breastbone revealed by the neckline of a blouse, a small diamond on a gold chain or a Tiffany heart. I imagined that she smelled of Gucci Rush, like poppers, like a baby's breath mixed with its mother's hairspray.

Helena told me that her sister just moved her food around the plate when she ate, suspected eating disorder, she was all skin and bones. I knew it, I knew she was skinny.

Helena told me that Olga was coming down to the city from school. Olga was supposed to spend the summer with her dad but the trip kept getting postponed, you never know, you just never know. Olga's final grades would be bad, Olga was going to do a gap year, she might do remote high school, that was one possibility, it had been a mistake to move to Sweden, everything was boring and sad here, time didn't move as it should. Helena wasn't able to see me anymore, or maybe she didn't want to, but she often called me late at night when she couldn't fall asleep, she wanted me to keep her company until she dozed off. I lay there like a person in love, with my phone on speaker as I listened to her wheezing breath and when she asked are you there? I replied: I'm here.

The calls stopped coming and I suspected this meant that Olga had come home, that she had replaced me. I suspected it was code red, that the family had closed its ranks, that I had become superfluous, undesired. I yearned for her to need me again.

MANY YEARS EARLIER I'd seen a show with photographs by Sophie Calle, a series called *The Last Picture*: portraits of people who'd gone blind, accompanied by their own descriptions of the last thing they saw before losing their sight, along with a second photograph, a reconstruction of the scene they described. A man in Istanbul, by the sea: "There is no final image—I lost my sight gradually—but the image that lingers, the one I miss: three children I can no longer see, sitting side by side, across from me, on the living room couch where you are currently sitting." In the reconstruction of this missed scene, the couch was empty.

There was an innocuous proximity to death in those images, the idea of being able to recount one final image, the last thing you saw in life. The photos filled me with a sort of enjoyable angst. I luxuriated in my feelings; I luxuriated in feeling bad for the blind, the distance between myself and them.

The show featured another photo that gave me no pleasure; years later it still filled me with horror. It portrayed the artist's mother on the beach, she was dying, I remembered the title as *The Last Journey*, I was unable to recall if it was a still image or a movie though I swore I could hear the sound of waves when I thought of it, I hadn't taken a picture. What I do remember, what I could never forget, were the words the artist's mother, according to the card next to the work, repeated again and again to herself as she sat dying on the beach: c'est bizarre, c'est bête.

The wall of that same room had a couple of sentences

printed on it that likewise have never left me, which over the years since then have come to feel like a verdict on my life. I didn't take a picture of them because I didn't want to remember, but they returned against my will and etched themselves within me, in a distorted version: "My mother wrote in her journal: my mother died today. Today it was my turn to write: my mother died today. Nobody will say those words about me."

When Helena's phone calls stopped I was overwhelmed by a desire to find the source of that text, to somehow disarm it, look it square in the face like exposure therapy for some fear or phobia, spiders, small spaces, a hope that the loneliness I'd experienced many years before would evaporate when I encountered the words again.

I went to Kulturhuset's library and found *Rachel, Monique*, the artist's book about her mother, which I believed to be the source of the text. But I couldn't locate the lines I'd been looking for, the ones I remembered; all I found was a page from the journal that used to belong to the mother, the Rachel, Monique in question, where it said: "Aujourd'hui ma mère est morte." I wondered if the text on the wall had been from something else, or if I'd added that last sentence myself, if my own memory had played a sentimental joke on me this whole time.

I WENT TO THE OPERA for a midday dance performance. I had no plans. I went to distract myself from something. The orchestra pit was shuttered and the fact that the lights were on in the auditorium made me feel awful, it was all wrong from the start, I wanted darkness and I wanted to feel outside of real life and real time, wanted the sensation of being asleep or at the airport. A dancer walked across the stage with a machine that displayed a digital message, in Swedish and English: VÄNLIGEN STÄNG AV ERA TELEFONER— PLEAS TURN OFF YOUR PHONES. I wondered if the misspelling was intentional, and the fact that I couldn't know only entrenched my misgivings and angst, feelings whose sources I couldn't identify when I tried, when I ransacked myself and my day up until that point.

I turned off my phone and the lights dimmed. The dancers were wearing almost no clothes. They resembled votive offerings, bodies like melting wax. They were pressed against a piece of glass that grew greasy, foggy. The formation brought to mind a mass grave. I started to imagine what it was like to be among them, the smells and the heat. It was not sexual. My interest was in the allusion to violence; that's where I wanted to participate. It was the sound of the dancers' feet against the floor, the skin against the glass, the pressure of the muscle, the hard bone just below.

Sitting there, I never lost track of time. Everything unfolded very slowly.

Afterward I stood for a long while on the stairs leading down to Gustav Adolf's square, the phone in my hand a cool, shiny stone while I waited for it to come back to life. My heart was thumping. I had been struck by a strong premonition that Helena had tried to call me right when I wasn't available. But there was nothing, nothing had changed in the short span of time I'd spent in the dark and I felt both relieved and disappointed, or maybe it was the same feeling I gave two different names. I messaged Josef. She's something special that choreographer isn't she, he replied, there's nobody like her.

I walked along the water; the rapids whirled furiously. I fantasized about the voice mail she hadn't left, imagined her telling me that her father was dead, imagined her saying: it was terrible, her voice resigned, he was afraid, she wished she'd never have seen his open eyes. I pictured scenes I'd seen in movies. I imagined the events that would ensue and which might very well already have occurred without my knowledge: plans made for his likely tasteful funeral, in lieu of flowers the family prefers donations to be made to some charity or research fund, white roses or calla lilies for the family members to hold.

Suddenly I realized, it was obvious, he was already dead; this was the reason for her silence. But to presume that, to reach out with condolences, it would be cruel if it weren't true. There was nothing I could do.

I missed Helena. I missed yet another family I did not belong to.

AT ONE POINT in the summer that followed, Olga and I almost met.

Her school semester had ended. She was about to travel to see her dad. Helena had told me that she and Olga were going to Ermoupoli at the end of the summer, to get away from everything, they were going to stay there for several weeks together, and I felt lonely and embittered but still looked forward to a summer with her, summer in the city, she was going to be in town just like me. Olga wasn't going back to school that fall. Nothing was working. Helena told me about the funeral, Olga hadn't worn a black dress, she'd chosen an oversized suit instead and with her thin neck and shaved head she looked like she was playing dress-up, like a child standing on another child's shoulders, Helena told me, not without pride, that her sisters must have thought she looked mad. Her nieces were in identical black wrap dresses, I think my sister bought them, can you imagine, she buys clothes for her adult children, she doesn't let them find their own identity, Helena felt bad for them. They had cried more than anybody else, they had cried the way small children and abandoned people do, there was snot. She repeated: Olga wasn't going back to school. Olga was going to come to Ermoupoli with her. She was going to figure something out, remote schooling maybe, a year off maybe, perhaps an evaluation, she's not well. But sun is the best cure, and rest, and now, soon, both of them were going to get some good rest.

Sometime after this conversation, before Olga had left to spend time with her dad, Helena called and invited me over for dinner. Her voice was oddly quiet, as if she was concerned that someone was listening. Come keep us company, she said, why don't the three of us have dinner together. It was the only time I declined an invitation from her.

I had no explanation for my hostility. None other than jealousy. It wasn't rational; I couldn't bear the thought of meeting her daughter. The thought of their intimacy was too frightening; it made the intimacy Helena and I had seem fragile. I said no.

I knew it made her angry that I declined, the only time I said no, because the next time we saw each other, after Olga had left, she was quiet, curt, I spent all night in her studio, looking at her books, I studied Herbert List's photograph of two boys in cheap paper masks, side by side and super-imposed on each other like a hologram, they were holding something in their hands, a crab or a shell or a rock, they might have been one and the same person. Their boundaries were at once sharp and dissolved; the only clearly defined part of their bodies was where they met.

I know that our bond intensified when I said no since it proved what I was capable of: I could leave her. I had shown her that she needed me. I had shown her that she'd miss me and I was the unavailable one, not her. Maybe this no was the precondition for my meeting Olga later, in Ermoupoli, for the invitation that came. Impossible to know, dizzying to imagine.

Later on I would think of this meeting that never took place, of another version of my life where everything could have gone differently. I could have met Olga earlier. I could have met Olga later. Each version had its own suffering, its own happiness. The few months that separated our first meeting from this hypothetical meeting stretched into a mass of time that made it seem like the Olga I met in early September was nothing like the Olga I could have met in early June. There might have been some truth to this feeling. In June she was still linked to phenomena I associated with childhood: time structured around school semesters, parents. But in September, when I met her in the garden in Ermoupoli, she was alone.

3.

❧ Orion ❧

JOSEF AND ALAIN'S RELATIONSHIP HAD left a trace on my body that was more permanent than any traces of my own relationships: a constellation on the sole of my right foot. A stick-and-poke we'd made one evening after we found the needles in a kitchen drawer while looking for something else, a lighter; the needles were Alain's. He'd forgotten about them. I imagined that at this point they'd probably been left behind in Josef's apartment, imagined that his belongings were strewn across the home and that Josef would keep coming across them in the ensuing years; I imagined that the reminders of their life would crop up over time like archaeological findings. Alain always scattered his things about and never installed himself fully during the time they lived together; he seemed to be perpetually unpacking and organizing his belongings in great haste, always rushing as if he were going somewhere and didn't have time to pause and decide where to put his stuff so he could find it later when he needed it, and this was what had happened with the needles, he'd forgotten about them altogether, he'd brought them when he moved in and then forgotten about them. At their rediscovery they suddenly seemed very valuable and he was excited, fascinated; he wanted a memory of dubious hygiene. Josef marked the motif, the dots, the stars, with a ballpoint pen. He left the room when

Alain got started; he couldn't bear to watch the needle going in.

Alain had a bunch of random tattoos, like a tough guy in a Jean Genet novel, but on his body they had the opposite effect, they made him look soft and pretentious, dated. Anchors, roses, hearts overlaid with banners. He looked like he was wearing a costume. His shins were striated by pale scars from cutting but not his arms, he never followed through on anything.

Alain had become obsessed with something he'd heard, which was that Fassbinder had wanted to make a movie based on *Giovanni's Room*. He couldn't stop talking about this nonexistent film, this film which would never be more than an idea. Talking about it made him so excited he sounded angry: just imagine the scenery, the shadows, imagine the oysters in Les Halles; he was fixated on that particular scene, the thought of oysters, he thought they were disgusting, the image of oysters in fiery technicolor light, the slime, the gleam, the stack of shells. He did not eat oysters. He said: it tastes like cunt. I said: no. Get a grip. It annoyed me when he talked like this; I knew that Josef also got annoyed when Alain's clowning sometimes cut through his customary aggressive somberness, but there were times when Josef loved that humor, when he told me: honestly it's kind of the only thing we have in common, we really like to laugh, and I hated them both.

The view of the needle piercing my skin entranced me, the ink that dried; I too was overcome by fascination, silence settled around us, all I could hear was his breathing. I had no sensation; there was no memory of pain. That's when Josef left the room. But before stepping out he turned around and for a second right then I met his eyes, and I was struck by a sense that something deeply inappropriate was going on, that Alain and I were somehow violating him.

AS HELENA AND I were walking the distance between the bus and the rocky beach, she told me about a memory, a memory of her father. She told me it came back to her when she saw the sea down the steep hill where we walked.

It was the first time she'd mentioned her dad since early summer. While she talked I got the impression that she hadn't shared this memory with anyone in a long time, or maybe ever. It was as if she was trying out a narrative, the definitive story of who he'd been. She said: my dad always had all these antics. My dad was always very stubborn. That's who he was. This memory was a story from back when they were still close, before she became a teenager and before her never-ending rage, a time when she did not yet have any other gods.

They were on vacation in the late 1960s. A road trip through Europe. She was too young to remember the exact route, but as far as she could recall they traveled far and were gone for a long time; her memory of this trip was that it had lasted all summer, an entire season, even if she'd understood later that this couldn't be true. On their way down south or back up north they stopped at Møns Klint in Denmark. Had I ever been? No. She would show me a picture later. In any case, Møns Klint were some highly unusual cliffs. White cliffs. Her dad had made the entire family, her mom, her sisters, go see them.

Actually, no—Helena changed her mind. Her youngest sister wouldn't have been born by then. And her other sister would have been very young, a baby. Maybe her mother had stayed behind with the sister in the car. But the memory was clear; in her mind the entire family had been there and everyone was scared of going up the cliffs, and her dad had gone to the very edge, close to the point where the ground just dropped, with no fence, where the trees grew straight up in defiance of gravity, and he'd roared: this is a memory for life! He raged at the family, who didn't see it. She was laughing as she recounted the story for me.

And finally, she said, I did find the courage to get up there, I was the only one who did. She was back in the version of her memory that included the entire family. And she remembered that her father had picked her up, even though she would have been a little too old to be held at that point; it might have been the last time in her life that her father carried her. And then she saw, through the trees, the rock face down below, it was white like marble, and she saw the water, which was turquoise like the Mediterranean, turquoise like in Greece, where she would travel several years later. And it was true, it was a memory for life.

ONE MORNING I heard Helena tell Olga: a mother is someone a child can share everything with. I was in the kitchen and seemingly out of earshot, which made me think that her statement was significant since she'd wanted to hide it from me. She didn't use the words "me" and "you," and Olga didn't reciprocate with a confidence but gave her, instead, a drawn-out, lightly sarcastic "Mmm." I didn't know what Helena wanted Olga to tell her; maybe she didn't know either.

One morning I heard them quarrel. I hadn't left my room and they were on the ground floor. I stayed put, didn't dare to leave, not until I heard Olga stomping up the spiral staircase and shutting the door behind her. I kept my distance. I never asked either of them what it was about and I'm not sure either of them could have remembered anyway. I felt envious of the way they yelled at each other: they yelled like people who loved each other, people who could never escape each other.

HELENA WOKE UP with a headache. She was grim at breakfast, the coffee made her feel nauseous, the buzzing of the flies sounded like machine guns. She didn't want to go to the beach. She didn't want to do anything. Her morning rest in the sarcophagus dragged on into the afternoon and I tried to tend to her—a cold towel? a glass of water?—but my desire to assist seemed to annoy her and I felt subservient and embarrassed. I hid, like Olga, in my room. On the balcony I watched the boats and the sea. A disquiet bloomed, in my throat, over my skin like a rash, a current in my body; I recognized the feeling but told myself I was mistaken, it was nothing. This was not rejection taking shape.

I went grocery shopping, I made mussels, her favorite. I took my time knocking the shells against the coarse stone edge of the sink, I proceeded slowly, I made my movements small. I lit the lanterns on the table in the garden when dusk fell. Helena drank a glass of white wine with ice in it. Olga took a piece of bread and slid it around the plate with olive oil. A hard, forceful silence I didn't understand rose from both of them. Olga left the table, she almost hissed, thanks for cooking, as if it were a secret code only she and I knew.

Go to bed, I told Helena. I tried to sound authoritative and merciful. I'll take care of this. She rubbed her temples, she opened her eyes wide, her mouth was straight and broad, she resembled a death mask. Is it a migraine? No, just the heat, the humidity, nothing in particular. None of your fucking business. She laughed, strained. Kidding. She was just so tired.

She had no energy to talk. I left her in the garden, where she leaned back with her glass of wine, staring at the wall.

The following morning she woke full of energy. She got up while Olga and I were still sleeping, she'd already been to the ferry office to get a timetable, she'd bought midnight-colored cherries marinated in syrup, you need to try these. A sweetness that burned and stung. Olga stuffed her mouth full and her teeth squeaked as she chewed. You're real sleepyheads, aren't you, I've been up since—, and the weather was perfect, a bit windy but not too bad, a nice breeze from the sea. She knocked on the timetable with one finger: we should go on an excursion, what do you think. We should go to Delos. It was possible to make it a day-trip, the first ferry to Mykonos, the boat from there, we could be back the same evening. We could stay overnight at Mykonos but that was for later, when it was bearable, when the clubs began to close down for the season, when the tourists had left. Not us. We'll see, she said. She'd circled the departures with a pencil and the marks had smudged, sooty shadows over the times. Delos, she said, solemnly. She wanted to see Delos again. She wanted to show us. The lions, the columns, the headless human statues. Archaeologists were the only ones allowed to spend the night on the island, she thought it was so romantic, it had been her childhood dream job, archaeologist. She smacked her lips, her teeth almost chattering with excitement. But not today, we weren't going to do it today. Today she wanted to be alone.

I was glad to see her in such a cheerful mood, it made me

relieved, the feeling was almost overwhelming. She wanted to be alone, I could understand that, or rather, I thought to myself: I can understand that she wants to be alone. I didn't protest. I waited for her to come back.

ERMOUPOLI WAS STILL a name that made me dream. It was foreign and romantic, more an idea than a physical place where I'd found myself. I'd been struck by a similar sensation when visiting places called "historical" or places I'd read about—forests, certain cities—where the real-life original never seemed as real as their narrated counterparts.

Helena didn't retreat; she went out instead. She left the house to be alone. I did as she did. I went on long walks without a map, with no goal other than having something to tell her when she came home at night; I didn't want her to think I was bored, that I was idle, that I had nothing to do. I wanted to conquer the city. I wanted to immediately familiarize myself with this place Helena and Olga had known for so many years. With our house as a starting point I navigated based on the buildings and streets I already knew—the city hall, the commercial streets that linked the square with the harbor, the restaurants, the library with the mayoral busts, contemporary people in marble. I walked through the cathedral park attached to the Church of Saint Nicholas, the church of Santa Claus, patron saint of the city and children, of prostitutes and remorseful thieves. The asphalt reverberated through my knees. I committed the names to memory, the beautiful names: Asteria's bar by the sea, Vaporia. I looked at the luxury hotels and the old shipping-magnate villas that seemed to pitch straight into the sea. I walked above the docks, all the way to the edge, to the last street before the sea, a pine grove on the hillside. At the end of the houses I saw a black cat in the brush, a computer with a cracked screen on the ground, an aloe vera plant covered in so many snails that I mistook them for flowers. Retracing my steps I saw black cats everywhere, everywhere I turned, and something about it felt absurd.

Outside one of the city's many abandoned buildings I noticed a strange detail. This house was situated on one of the streets that ran between the city hall and Helena's house. It was big, imposing but decrepit. It had a tall iron gate, it had holes in the facade where the plaster had fallen away in large chunks, the sky was visible behind the wooden blinders. Always, every time I walked down that street, there were ten or so plastic bottles filled with water lined up along the wall. I'd observed something similar at the fish-monger, plastic bags filled with water to keep birds and flies away since the reflecting light scared them. I never saw any-body when I walked past that house, but I did notice that the bottles sometimes changed places and I assumed that someone went there to add water as it evaporated. The pi-geons who huddled in flocks on the cornices of the surround-ing buildings never landed on that house, and the piles of cats lounging in the shadows thrown by the walls of other buildings never came near it either. I never saw these bot-tles by any other building. It was an odd sign of life, one ac-tually meant to repel life, a strange act of care for this lost palace.

When I described the house to Helena she knew exactly what I was talking about. The building had looked like that for as long as she could remember, it was already crumbling fifteen years ago, sooner or later it'll collapse, a safety risk, someone should do something about it. I soon discovered that the city was full of houses like this, abandoned structures with gates shuttered by chains, heavy padlocks restraining decaying doors, windows gaping empty behind bars. Some appeared to have been left in a rush, desolate scenes through a window: a vanity with an old, hazy mirror, a clock that had forever stopped at 11:14, its second hand at number 10, photographs on the wall. There was one house where you could peek in between the collapsed walls and glimpse a pantry full of bottles, all of them old, some with labels I couldn't read but most of them anonymous, tall, transparent glass with porcelain corks, their contents yellow and waxy, thick, eerie. It looked like nobody had set foot there in a century.

Sometimes these abandoned buildings frightened me; I was scared to look through the bars, suddenly superstitious, I imagined that a chill surrounded the area, paranormal clichés.

After a while I realized what I hadn't seen even once during my long, aimless walks: a cemetery. At the end of the nineteenth century the city had a population double the size of today's, which made me think that the dead should be more numerous than the living. But where were they? Helena had no answer when I asked. It was strange, she said, because she really loved cemeteries. I really love cemeteries, she said, I really love cemeteries. She enjoyed walking among the mausoleums at the Northern Cemetery in Stockholm. Her favorite was Paul U. Bergström's family grave, the copper door and the star, we should go see it someday, you and I. She would have known if they had something like that here. You'd imagine they'd have had the resources to build beautiful resting places for the dead who lived their lives in the villas by the sea. But I found no such monuments, not even a site for simple graves, no memorial grove in the little park in front of Saint Nicholas Church where the cats slept in the shade of the pine trees.

THE DAYS WERE hot, white. We waited for the night and a respite that never came with it; we drank our wine lukewarm, muscles loosened from the bone like boiled meat, smells washed over us in warm waves, bay leaves, trash, sand, and all the while the boats bellowed lazily in the distance.

Helena wanted to eat light foods, tomato salad with lots of vinegar. She no longer took honey with her breakfast; I suspected she was dieting but trying to hide it from me. She asked me to boil eggs; she asked me to buy eggplant and lemon. I ran her errands in a state of impatience and hope; I often feared she'd have left by the time I came back and was overjoyed when she was still there, when she had waited for me.

We went back to the rocky beach. Helena asked Olga if she wanted to come; she said no. It was hot and hazy, the sun had no contours, Helena indicated a point on the horizon: when the weather is clear you can see all the way to Gyaros. Do you know what that is? The devil's island. She sounded excited, like she was telling a ghost story. Look! Gives me goose bumps. She showed me her arm, which appeared no different than normal. There used to be a prison camp there; they sent the prisoners to the hospital here in Ermoupoli to die.

Her face was wild when she talked about the island. The nature out there was so untouched, she said, it was no different from Homer's time. She dreamed of seeing it one day. There were no ferries; you had to know someone. She loved deserted places. It was eerie, a dark historical chapter. She squinted at the horizon. She pointed again in a different direction: actually it might be more that way, impossible to tell right now anyway. The sky was both compact and dissolved over the sea, as if the air was full of a fine white dust.

HELENA HAD a different way of talking when Olga was present. She used another voice, a voice she seemed to draw from a place within, and I thought of this as her family voice. The voice annoyed me as much as it made me feel sad, it made me feel lonely. Why had she never used it with me before? This voice was a bit forced, but beautiful, like she was doing a radio play. Like she was performing for Olga—suddenly, during one of our conversations around the dinner table, conversations Olga never took part in, she'd turn to her and pose a question, as if seeking some kind of validation I couldn't provide: isn't it true that I've always been this sloppy? I committed this question to memory because she wasn't asking about a positive trait, but apparently it was something she valued, and this was the type of knowledge you only gained after a long time of living with another person.

Olga's answers were often monosyllabic. Either she couldn't quite hide how bored these questions made her or else she wanted to project boredom. But there were moments when genuine excitement spread across her face—it made her beautiful, briefly uninhibited, childish—and she'd respond, emphatically: no, it's not at all—, and that transient expression hurt me almost more than Helena's voice.

HELENA DIDN'T BRING me to the rocky beach again, but it was only later that I realized it had been the last time, which meant I'd never stopped waiting for her. If I'd known, I'd probably have committed other things to memory, imbued the moment with a certain light or darkness, given myself a different feeling—anger, grief—than the stale disappointment that began to take root in me a week or so into my stay.

I walked. I found my routes. I rarely deviated from them; I started to walk in a set pattern: from the buildings to the harbor, down Chiou, I went shopping, I drank coffee at the city hall café. I preferred it to the cafés around the square because of how cool it was, because of the comfort of being among busy strangers, the sound of footsteps in the hallways overhead. It made me feel calm. I went swimming from the dock in Vaporia and it felt sinful, taboo to swim alone, to have found a place "of my own" which wasn't my own at all but which I had discovered without her help. My hair was still wet in the evening and I hoped she would notice and realize she missed me.

Later I would remember this lonely period of exploration, of charting the city on foot, as if it had gone on for weeks when in reality it was no more than a couple of days. When I was shown a map of Ermoupoli I understood that the city I had thought I'd covered completely was in fact far vaster than I'd known, that there were big sections of it I had never seen and hadn't taken into account; I thought I'd reached the city's outskirts when in actuality I'd been at the edge of areas I hadn't known existed. I saw that for the most part I'd been walking in circles in the same neighborhoods, the ones abutting Persefonis, which I'd mistaken for the city's center since it was the center of my existence when I was there. Memory had stretched my asymmetrical, searching routes and made them seem never-ending. Time wasn't logical. A span of time that felt, back then, in the beginning, like several weeks, was in fact just a few days. A span of time that felt, later, like a few days or even less, only a few brief moments, was in fact unfolding for much longer than that, enormous expanses of time that I greedily swallowed and demanded more of, which I couldn't get enough of, which I didn't want to end, which I wanted to stretch and become forever.

THE NIGHTS CREPT closer to day. At dusk, when I sat on the balcony and waited for the sound of Helena's footsteps approaching the house, there was an almost-imperceptible click when the streetlights came on and the skies became windy and blue. There was a smell of fried pork, gas, cat piss, rosemary, ash, saltwater, pink floor soap. When the ferry came or left—I could never tell which—it played a stubborn melody, a nursery melody, the repetitive sound of a certain kind of toy, plastic buttons, a toy for very young children. That sound made me feel sad and I couldn't explain why, aside from the obvious reasons: the association with childhood, the association with a farewell being repeated day after day, from morning to night.

THE FEELING of easy intimacy I'd experienced when I first came to Ermoupoli returned at night. During those hours everything was maybe not "like it used to be" but at least how I had dreamed of it being before I arrived, the way I'd pictured it: Helena and I alone at the table after Olga had gone to her room, we drank white wine, Tsipouro with ice, we smoked, it was warm in the garden even after darkness fell. I listened to Helena's stories. Behind her the house glowed like a lantern and I saw, out of the corner of my eye, the light from the lamp in the window on the second floor. Bugs flocked around the candles on the table, the remnants of our meal and the glasses; my feet were covered in little scabs I scratched up in my sleep, red bumps where the pus dried into amber pearls. These bites made me feel at home—I'd take them with me when I left, and a piece of me would stay behind, thousands of mosquitoes born out of my blood.

I sometimes got tired of Helena in the evenings, but in a satisfying and familiar way, the way I imagined an adult daughter might get tired of her mother. I got tired of her endless talking, her inability to get to the point or finish a story; whenever I tried to respond in some way she would interrupt me, especially when she was drunk. She raised her voice, she took a long time finding the right words. I fell into a kind of stupor where I no longer really listened. I let my gaze wander to the glowing window behind her. I had a thought, it seemed taboo: was this really what I had longed for, to sit across from this quite ordinary person? The thought made me feel satisfied. I felt rich when she went on like this. I felt calm: she wasn't going anywhere. She wasn't about to leave me.

The mornings broke with the return of painful uncertainty, a return of the past where I'd spend my days waiting for Helena's phone call. I was hoping for something, I felt like a child but no longer in a nice way. I set the breakfast table very slowly and with exaggerated care, as if I might extend the time when there was still a chance she'd want my company. Helena drank her coffee fast. Helena was going out for a bit. By then I had lost the game, time had run out, nothing I said or did could change the matter.

Olga and I were left behind, left over; I wondered if she felt that way too. I wanted to approach her somehow, get her assurance that my feelings were normal. I felt that we were somehow united, and I wanted her to realize that. I was impatient when she was close by. I was impatient when she wasn't under my supervision. Who knew what kinds of things she was thinking as she stayed back at the house while Helena and I were out.

I made myself busy to fend off the feeling of abandonment, the feeling of being a burden—I planned meals, I went out, I went to the sea—I staged a life as it would have looked if I were alone, but I didn't want to be alone.

THERE WAS A MAN I kept seeing on the dock in Vaporia; he was younger than the retirees who sat along the wall and listened to music from a CD player but older than me, he might have been Helena's age. He was always alone there, like me. I began to identify with him; I thought of him as a friend even though we'd not exchanged a word. I wasn't interested in talking to him. I imagined that his situation was like mine, that he was busy making himself busy, passing time waiting for something he hadn't quite been promised. I looked for him on the dock every time I arrived, and if he wasn't there I was beset by a vague anxiety that didn't ease until he showed up, and which otherwise, if he didn't appear, dogged me on the way home: why not today?

The man would often sit at the edge of the dock, slightly hunched as he stared at the sea. The first thing that made me notice him: his bandaged foot, which prevented him from going in the water. He limped. Whenever he got up to walk to and fro on the dock, his gait was irritable, as if he hadn't gotten used to the limp. His walk was jagged, hard, his foot angled inward as if he'd stepped on something sharp or on hot, glowing embers.

I liked to lie down close to the wall, in the shade of a big bush. Between the man and me, underneath the large parasol that bore into the center of the dock, a group of teen girls would sprawl in the afternoon. They rarely got in the water, they just sat there, sometimes playing music that competed with the retirees', but neither group seemed bothered by the other. The cats on the dock went back and forth between them, begging for something to eat, slinking against the girls, stretching out in the sun.

I could tell that the man had been beautiful at one point, or, rather: he was beautiful, but he was not young, and that made me think that his present beauty hid an even bigger, now-lost beauty. He was sinewy and short. He wore small black swim shorts, a golden chain around his neck that sparkled in the sun, and though he had onset baldness his chest hair was a cloud that almost seemed to hover an inch from his body. A testosterone look. I liked his stringiness and his dimensions. I enjoyed watching him from a distance, unseen: I'm just looking at the sea is what I would've answered if anyone asked me, but nobody ever did. I felt bad for the man because he couldn't swim. I recognized some of my own history in this body, which fumbled, struggling, as it moved over the dock. My own sympathy for the man, extended to him without his knowledge, made me feel kindly. A crushing thought sometimes flashed through my mind, and it was always followed by a repugnant feeling: that he truly was alone, not just on the dock, but absolutely, completely alone—a person who lived without ties to other people, a person who lived without God, without family, without friends, without sexuality, without pleasure. I wondered if he'd noticed me and if the same thought had struck him.

I used to envy men their straight bodies, their dense flesh, their dry sex, their sexuality, which seemed direct and sturdy. I envied their hardness. There was a softness between young women that I was aware of but had never experienced, a softness that had never come naturally to me: sleeping together, sharing a bathtub, the cheek against the shoulder, a head in the lap, hair like cat fur. The sweet waxy scent of lipstick, paint the lips, suck on a finger to remove the excess: kiss proof. I refused. I did not participate. Homosexuality made me terrified of homoeroticism. It was too real. Nothing is innocent when you have something to hide. I thought about the lonely man in Vaporia: maybe he's gay, maybe that's why I've noticed him.

ONE MORNING Helena ate the honey in her yogurt again, she swirled it around her spoon, she asked me to buy bread and tomatoes, that evening she wanted us to go out for dinner together. Olga did not want to join and Helena made no attempt to convince her. This irritated me, not because I wanted her company but because I didn't think it was right that she had the choice and also, partly, due to a complicated sort of jealousy: the ease with which she said no to a person I wanted to be close with irritated me.

As if she had read my mind, Helena explained to me, as soon as we were alone, that Olga's dad had given her *Steppenwolf* that summer, and this book had made her ill-mannered. Helena didn't like the book, she didn't like that the dad had given it to Olga, who does he think she is, some guy, a cineaste in a beret, he really has no soul, it's tone-deaf, honestly. Helena didn't like the way Olga said "I love you" on the phone to her dad. In English it sounded tasteless and fake, like a line from a movie.

For as long as I'd known her, Helena had been circumspect about her marriages, the first one in particular, which she only referred to as a span of time—"this was when I was married to my first husband; this was two years after I'd married . . ."—she never said his name when she talked about him. As for the second marriage, the one to Olga's father, she sometimes hinted that there was a story there that she was hiding from me, that there was something seriously wrong with him, that he was crazy, that he was violent. She used words that could be euphemisms: he was particular, he was strong-willed. Almost every time, including now, she got angry when he came up, and her uninhibited way of expressing this anger made it seem justified. Most of the time her hints left me with the sense that I was being misled, that her inscrutability was a question of hiding not a dark truth, just a boring one: she'd once been married to a person she no longer loved. I wondered if she missed his last name, which Olga still bore. I wondered if she envied Olga's natural bond to this man the way I envied Olga's natural bond to Helena.

"Oneiro" means "dream," Helena told me; it was the name of the restaurant: beautiful, isn't it.

We ate ice cream with mastic and poppy seeds. In the backyard where we sat, lamps were strung between the leafy walls and the sky overhead was warm, taut like a tablecloth. It looked expensive, that sky, the walls and the leaves, the cool on the tongue and the taste of resin, metallic and ancient. We ate from the same spoon, passing it back and forth. Aside from a family of four, we were the restaurant's only guests. The others were sitting at a remove from us and I couldn't tell what language they were speaking but they looked like sailors to me, which is to say wealthy, which is to say tourists like us, though Helena, I knew, did not think of us in that way. Tourist: a guest with bad taste.

I felt tense. I couldn't quite relax during dinner, I drank a lot of wine, I couldn't focus on what Helena was saying and had to ask her to repeat herself several times. I realized I was waiting for something—an explanation, the true reason she wanted to go for dinner—a message that would crush me; it felt like I was waiting to be destroyed. I experienced the situation the way I had experienced dates where it was obvious to both of us that the reason for our meeting was to break up. But Helena and I had never been romantically involved, which meant that our relationship would never end in such a clinical, definitive way. The thought gave me no comfort.

We had both had quite a bit to drink, I lit her cigarette and sensed the contours of a feeling—of pain, of eroticism, or neither, just something that reminded me of them. You should stop smoking, she said. It's one thing for someone of my generation, but you're so young . . .

The sounds of the family reached us now and then in bursts, the melody of the unfamiliar language punctured by shrill laughter. A man, a woman, a son, a daughter, their ages probably in that order; having spent a couple of hours in their proximity I now felt as if I'd seen through this family's dynamics completely, and I had begun to hate all four of them. The dominance of the mother, her authoritative and entitled manner; the father, passive-aggressive and critical, cold, unimpressed by the food, the company, the setting, this vacation he was enduring, this domain he disliked; he made me sad. The voices of their son—he had multiple, he was putting on an act, talking loudly—more piercing than the others', unbearably affected. His sister's giggling was out of control.

The son annoyed me even as I felt tender toward him. He wasn't doing his voices to entertain but to save himself; he is hiding something, I thought, he wants validation. He only got it from his younger sister, her braying, which climbed the walls, skyward; her laughter wasn't worth anything, she gave it up too easily.

Sitting near them made me feel isolated and lonely. They

made me uncomfortable with their unhappiness. I wondered what assumptions they made about me and Helena. A mother and her daughter? Friends? I wondered what they saw and what was visible on me. I wondered in what ways they thought they'd figured us out, what seemed obvious from their horizon.

I WENT TO SIT in the garden after we came home. Helena went to bed. I drank a glass of wine from a bottle that had been left out in the kitchen all day and was now warm. It was oily like pool water, sweetish. At night the sounds grew stronger and more remote, the engines, the voices in the distance, as if in a hangar. I allowed thoughts to enter my mind however they wanted, like waves breaking on the shore. I thought about the water that goes on and on, expanding and circulating even as life ends. I thought about star constellations. A sentence from Étienne Daho's Swedish Wikipedia page: "He lived a relatively careless life by the sea while the Algerian war was ongoing."

I pictured an octopus swimming through the darkness. I saw its heavy head, I saw its tentacles pushing off against the void, it was an image that had no sound whatsoever. It recurred later when I was about to fall asleep. The room was warm and my sheets were scratchy. Drunkenness pulled through my body like booming thunder. I saw the head and the tentacles when I shut my eyes, like a memory, a pulsing movement, steady like the beating of a heart.

AFTER THAT NIGHT I made a decision: I would need to leave very soon. The thought arrived effortlessly, more or less without my involvement, like a revelation. I saw that I was nearing the moment when I'd overstayed my welcome and I wanted to preempt it. Could I not take a hint, did I not realize that Helena didn't want me there—monotonous thoughts without question marks. I had arguments with myself—I wasn't a mind reader, after all; I shouldn't torture myself needlessly— but my shame at the thought of her actually reprimanding me, asking me to leave, showing me the door, was so powerful it convinced me. I would need to leave very soon.

Still, it wasn't easy. I was disappointed. I burned with the feeling that this trip wasn't what I'd expected, paired with the humiliation of realizing that I had expected something in the first place, something I hadn't been able to put into words. I hated being wrong. I'd thought it would be different.

Then again, there was solace in the thought of going back home, an anchor in the uncertainty that had beset me for several days. I wouldn't just up and leave; I was trying to figure out a polite date. I wasn't going to tell them I was leaving until the day before, maybe the night before, in order to show Helena that I'd made this decision independently of her and that nothing she did could make me change my mind. I was planning to pretend that I had always known when I was leaving; I didn't want it to seem like I was skulking off from Ermoupoli in humiliation.

It made me sad to think about the name of the city: it belonged to them, not me.

I WENT INTO the garden that morning, Helena had already left, I sat down with Olga. She was on her phone, her legs folded close to her chest and her feet on the seat of the garden chair, her toes curled over the edge, so deeply focused that it almost seemed like she was making an effort to not move at all as I walked around the table. I noticed a scar over one of her knees that I'd never seen before, an irregular freshwater pearl. It disappeared inside the folds of her skin when she put her leg down. She went to get her sketch pad. I made coffee.

My decision made me calm. It allowed me to enjoy the silence between us and the sounds in the garden, the sounds of life lived outside of our world, kids in the schoolyard down the block, their screeching rising like a thousand birds, the teacher's shrill whistle telling them it was time for class, their voices fading.

After a while she asked me, using a tone I'd never heard before, not the girlish one she had when responding to Helena, but a darker version: do you want to split an orange? I said yes, I'd love to. She went to get one and peeled it with her stubby fingers, a long orange spiral. A vague tenderness grew in me as I watched her hands move, a spark of joy when she cleaved the orange in two and passed me one of the halves. I said thank you and she said you're welcome. She didn't say anything else and I didn't say anything else either. We ate the fruit, we licked our fingers, it was truly delicious, so sweet and at the same time so bitter.

I CALLED JOSEF. I wanted to hear his voice. It took many rings before he answered; I could barely hear what he said because of the wind where he was, which sounded like a scream. He told me he was walking on a bridge, it probably sounds worse than it is, he said, how are things there, good. It's windy at night here too, I said. He asked me if it was warm. Yes. There was something soft about him that made me think we'd aged. I thought of all the parts of me that he had, all the things that were hidden, things we'd lost and would never find again; I grew melancholic as we spoke, the distance and the difficulty hearing him.

I was lying on the bed in my room, watching the net in front of the balcony ripple in the breeze. The door was open to the landing that separated my room and Olga's. I spoke in a quiet voice and he couldn't hear me well; I kept having to repeat myself. Cats, I said, cats everywhere, he thought I said "canals everywhere" and pictured Venice. You should come here sometime, you'd love it. There are swimming spots in the middle of town, just like Stockholm. And so beautiful, just different. As we spoke I caught myself creating a distance between us, inadvertently: my descriptions did not match my feelings, they were like a memory even though I was still in the middle of it. Good food? Yeah, lots of fish, lots of parsley . . . I had seen okra at the market, his favorite, but it turned out I'd misunderstood: it was Alain who loved okra, Josef thought it was slimy, I've always thought it was gross, he said. His emphatic tone made me unhappy. I felt lonely. If it was possible that I, despite all these years, despite our long friendship, had been wrong about this detail, then there might be other things, more meaningful pieces of information, that I had similarly believed with absolute certainty but which I'd misunderstood or never known. I got mixed up, I said.

I didn't want to tell him I was coming home.

I wished he'd have asked. I'd have liked to say: I don't know, I could stay here forever, easily.

I didn't know what to say, and neither of us spoke for a long while. The wind had faded on his end, but I still heard the city sounds through my phone, the outdoor sounds, the time sounds, like I was holding a shell to my ear. He had to go. I said, yeah, me too. For me it wasn't true.

After he hung up and the other city's sounds stopped, the sounds outside my own wide-open window returned; the world I'd left for the duration of our call came back. I heard the floor creak on the landing outside my door. Turning my head I caught a glimpse of Olga's back as she slipped into her room and carefully shut the door, making no sound. She'd heard me, I thought; she'd huddled out there listening to me—listening for what? A clue about the bond between us, the one I had sensed a couple of days earlier?

KNOWING THAT I would soon be going home made me attentive. I took my farewell; I was emotional, sentimental. I saw everything as if for the last time, since I believed it was the last time. No more hopes, no more "later." When I went out—I was picking up a couple of things, I was going swimming, suddenly it was all very laden with significance—I took another route to the sea than the one I'd gotten used to. I ended up in a cul-de-sac, I had to climb a set of stairs, figure out a different way. And there, like some kind of omen, on a street I'd never again find my way back to, I came across a garden that was eerily similar to Helena's. The house it belonged to was uninhabited, and green weeds lined the cracks in the stone wall. There was an orange tree whose location was the same as hers in her garden but it was much bigger, with warty fruits hanging from the branches and an unwieldy crown that cast its shade on the street. I stood by the low fence and listened to the mopeds nearby, their humming so close I kept thinking they were passing right behind me; music from an open window, the clanking of porcelain, a man who kept clearing his throat and coughing and clearing his throat. It was lunchtime.

Life was everywhere, but the garden was swept in a stillness so complete that it seemed like time didn't exist there. It was as if I were looking at Helena's house in the future, as if I'd returned twenty or forty years later to seek it out and found it deserted, the trees taller and older, the roof collapsed, plants having broken through the stone, not a single trace of our time spent there.

Perhaps the mood I was in exaggerated the similitude between this garden and Helena's. Since I never saw it again,
I couldn't check. It might have been like thinking that two
people are alike when you first meet and later, once you know
them better, once you're better acquainted with their finer
aspects, it's incomprehensible that you ever thought they
resembled each other. Perhaps it didn't matter—what appealed to me in this future scenario was the desolation, the
fact that it would be impossible to say to whom everything
had once belonged.

WHEN I CAME back to the house, Olga was not in the garden, and when I went upstairs to hang my wet towel over the balcony railing I noticed that the door to her bedroom was open. I couldn't resist the temptation to go in. If not now, when? I had never seen the room before and soon I would never see it.

A striking detail, her bed: washed-out stains of blood on the sheets.

The room was small. There was a dresser, but she didn't seem to make use of it: a suitcase lay open on the floor, her stuff spewing from it, clothes, books, earphones. The sweet fragrance of sweat lay in the air.

One of the room's two windows, the one whose glow I would watch in the evenings, was shut. The other was open to a little landing, the fire escape. I called out; no answer. I looked at the garden through the closed window. It was blurry with the glass as intermediary, a dream. I called her name again, yelling as loud as I could, and this time I thought I heard her voice responding from some indeterminate point above. When I climbed through the open window and up the fire escape, the sunlight forced me to blink. There she was, on the roof: lying belly down on a towel, dressed in a bikini, resting her chin in her fists. She looked like she'd been waiting for me in that position.

I sat down by her side, cross-legged. You scared me, I said, and it was only when I uttered the words that the images came, the fear that had gripped me the moment I saw her open door: that she'd disappeared, that something had happened to her, that the moment I came home from my swim and stepped through the door would have come to represent the final moment of innocence, before something life-changing took over. Close call.

Beneath my shirt my swimsuit was still damp, cutting into my groin. Olga sat up. Is my mom home? No. She seemed relieved by this information: she lay down again, on her back, put her head in her hands, arms stretched in a triangle. The hair in her armpits was dark and wild and shiny with sweat, like seaweed. I asked if she'd let me stay for a while. I wanted to look at the view. OK, she said, the word split into its letters the way I'd heard Helena say it: Oh Kay. There's something on your foot.

I looked. I didn't understand and thought she was teasing me. I found my feet embarrassing, they were dusty from walking in sandals, unevenly tanned, ugly from the crimson mosquito bites. Thick, raised veins ran across them like river deltas.

She put out her hand and touched my sole. There. A startling jolt of pleasure coursed through me. She said: you've got a stain.

I looked where she'd indicated. It wasn't a stain, it was a star, one single star remained from the tattoo Josef had drawn several years earlier. I hadn't thought about it in a long while. I hadn't noticed that the other stars had faded or worn off beneath my feet. I told her. Which constellation? I could no longer recall. I realized that I might never have known. I said I could find out for her. Please.

She closed her eyes against the sun. It made her look so innocent, a little troubled; the thick eyebrows shaded her eyelids. I sat by her side and regarded the sea and the sky that surrounded us, the sun, the clouds, the horizon vaulting itself in front of me.

I WROTE TO JOSEF; I didn't call him again. Do you remember? There's only one star left. I didn't want to stir his memory of the night he drew it, that is to say my own memory, the memory of his look; I wanted to make a new memory for the two of us, one that belonged to our history instead of his and Alain's history. He replied immediately. He hadn't thought of it in forever but he'd never forgotten: he got the exact same tattoo, on the same place but on his left foot, so that we'd be like two parts of the same body. He wrote: so dumb. You don't remember?

No, I didn't remember. I didn't understand how it was possible. It made me want to weep: that what I'd thought was the trace of a betrayal was in fact a sign of our friendship, one we'd carried together for several years.

His tattoo, he wrote, had faded a long time ago. They represented Orion.

I searched the image and saw a body with a bow and arrow. I read: Orion is one of few constellations where many of the stars are actually near each other in space. I found a painting: Orion, blinded, is looking for the sun; I read: Orion, a giant hunter who lost his sight and got it back from Helios, the sun, thanks to the power of love.

Reading this made me happy, the thought of a sun, unrequitedly in love, in ancient Greece. It made me sad, too, to think of the blinded Orion walking around looking for someone who loved him.

4.

❧ Echo ❧

THEY WERE RESTORING THE DOME ON the Church of Saint Nicholas. It was encircled by scaffolding, and backlit by the afternoon sun it resembled a magpie's nest. The stranger in Vaporia had a new cast: green. He still limped, he walked with the same jagged step, he dipped his healthy foot in the water sometimes when he sat on the edge of the dock, up and down like he was making a wax candle.

Olga accompanied me to the sea. The way she moved and talked changed the farther we got from the house. She grew more lively. She flung her arms about, making me conscious of the distance or proximity between our bodies: she kept almost touching me, all it would take was a small miscalculation of this distance or proximity.

Olga had a weird way of talking. Her international childhood made her seem a bit daft. It was neither an accent nor a dialect; I had never heard someone talk like that before. It followed no logic, her tongue wasn't where it was supposed to be, her sounds came out long and deep. The way her tongue touched her front teeth, as if she was about to attack. Her way of eating the words.

In our conversations she tended to ask questions, something I wasn't used to. I tossed them back and her response was almost exclusively: dunno. The things she asked me: polite, trivial questions, they could've been cribbed from a language-learning book. What's your favorite color. What's your favorite movie. How would you describe a perfect day. A day where everything happens and I don't have to do anything to make it happen, I told her, and I immediately felt that I'd revealed too much; how about you. Dunno. Would you rather be blind or deaf?

There was something in her I recognized. I got the impression that she was used to hiding parts of herself; it was her sweeping ways, her tendency to keep asking things, like she was diffracting attention from herself.

On the dock we were pursued by a cat without a nose, like a statue. She meowed and rubbed herself against our legs; we couldn't shake her. Dirty fur. I might have petted her were it not for the open nose, which grossed me out, a red, shiny dent in the center of the cat's face, like the skin beneath a blister. The teen girls under the parasol fed her chips. They shooed her away. She came back to us by the low wall in the sun; she pushed her face against Olga's naked belly. The majority of the street cats were incredibly cautious; they ran off as soon as you got close even though they were always surrounded by people. Not this one; it must have been starved for love. Go away, Olga said, we don't have any food, and she said it in such a crass, direct way that it made me laugh: she was talking to the cat as if it were a person.

I felt I saw something new in her in this moment. Olga often employed the disinterested tone of voice of someone who actually cares too much, someone who labors to subdue their sincerity, their feelings; she always gave herself away, something would seep out, in her eyes, in her voice, in the brevity of her sentences. Go away; she said it without timidity. Without her normal hesitation. But I liked her hesitation;

I saw myself in it. I wanted to tell her: I'm like you, we're not like other people, we're like each other.

She wanted to listen to music. She did not want to swim in the sea. She hugged her knees with her skinny arms. Her stomach creased. The sunshine made her bikini top sparkle, it smelled of chlorine, it flattened her breasts, it was too small, sporty, swimwear for school: swim five hundred yards, water safety and rescue training at ten feet. The teen girls wore different kinds of swimsuits, colorful, fashion wear. Climbing up the ladder I saw that she was gazing their way with a look I couldn't interpret: longing, maybe, or disdain.

WE ATE PERSIMMONS by the water. I let her pick a fruit at the market and persimmon was her choice. A childish fruit, I thought, "exotic," different, not a regular orange or pear. An odd shape, an odd name. We were handed the fruits in a yellow bag that smattered and rustled in the wind. The sun made the peels warm and slimy, hard to bite, the flesh slimy, nauseatingly sweet, black seeds like flecks of vanilla. My hands were salty, rough.

Olga's lips gleamed. She ate the fruit with a joy that both frightened and fascinated me: it had been a long time since sugar inspired such strong feelings in me.

I touched her scar. It was slippery next to the dry skin around it. What happened here, I said. A firecracker, she told me, using the English word, and she spread her legs to show me, on the inside of her thigh, a bigger scar, an archipelago of shiny skin. Firecracker? I wasn't familiar with the term in that language. She explained. I could have been disfigured, she said, sounding like she was repeating something adults had told her many times before. I could have gone blind. Did it hurt? She couldn't quite remember. It was cold at first, then hot, her skin had melted into her tights—she emphasized "melted," and "tights," like she was trying to convince me, she sounded both disgusted and tickled when she told me—but she didn't remember pain, she didn't remember it at all.

Her skin was so firm and smooth, it made me self-conscious. I pulled my knees up against my chest the way she did to stretch my own skin, feeling my body's looseness, gravity pulling on the flesh. I felt old next to her; I didn't want to be.

I liked Olga's scar. The rest would leave her in due time. The smoothness of her body, the specific beauty she had today. Only the scar would remain, would follow her, a souvenir from childhood.

I ENVIED THE EASE of the teens sitting under the parasol. It wasn't something I had felt before Olga joined me. I envied how close they were to her, that they were part of the same world; I envied them even though it wasn't a world I'd ever wanted to be part of. When I was their age I always wanted to get away from it. I wasn't attracted to girl stuff; none of it was interesting to me. Dolls, hair pins, mouths that smelled of milk, it disgusted me, all of it. I had no nostalgia for those years. I had no desire to return. It wasn't who I was. I wasn't stuck in childhood. I was never interested in kissing practice, in holding a spot until some man came along.

Olga's phone died in the sun. She played with her earphones, fiddled with the cord, it was broken, it had pencil marks on it. Do you miss your friends? She had none. I said: you'll get friends, later. You think so? She looked hopeful. Then she changed her mind: I don't want any friends. She didn't want to be part of any group. She was happier alone. She wanted to be herself. I heard you were depressed, I said, and she looked solemnly at me. No, she was just sad. She thought it was unfair that she wasn't allowed to do anything: live alone, for example. My mom is an idiot. She said it with an intensity that surprised me. She was dramatic: it's like prison, living with her. Is it really like a prison though, I said, you can do what you want after all; I think she seems fairly . . . and I couldn't finish the sentence because I didn't even know what I'd call it, that trait, Helena's independence, or solipsism, or hunger for freedom, which was what had left us two behind, left with each other. No, Olga said emphatically. I didn't want to come here with her. But here she was, and when Helena wanted to go home again she would follow, just as she would to wherever Helena wanted to go next. You've been coming here since you were born, right? Yes. She liked it more when she was younger. She said: when I was little I would sit in the water for hours pretending I was a sea monster, I didn't have to do anything, just pretend, I loved to sit there and think.

I thought of Helena's photo of her, the stony beach, the gaze, her naked body.

I asked if she would rather live with her dad. Dunno. My parents are so old, she said, nobody else has parents that old. I don't think that's true, I said. She didn't respond, just kept tugging at the cord, rolling it around her finger and unfurling it again.

I'm going to go back home soon, I said. You are? She sounded disappointed. I relished saying it; it felt like a trump card. Olga stretched out her legs; there were oceans of time before her. Olga wanted to be an adult. Olga hated Sweden, fir trees, bread, dullness. She didn't want to live there. She was bored. All she wanted to do was read, but not like they did in school, she said, her voice dripping with contempt: my textbooks had illustrations in them. I thought her disdain was funny. You've got your entire life to do that, I said, and there was a muted pang, the distance between us growing when I told her. She had something I didn't have. She had so many things I didn't have.

The man with the bandage was up and now he walked

past us, very close, on stiff legs; he was smoking a cigarette. I wondered if he remembered me. I wondered if he recognized me when I wasn't alone. I wondered what he thought we were. A mother and her daughter? Friends?

THE HEAT WAS stifling and white, the air hazy, slick; Olga's eyes were shiny. She wanted to pause on the way back, she needed to drink something. She had a tummy ache. She was dragging her feet. My hair was a heavy blister at my neck, I squeezed it when we passed the square, a stream of saltwater dripping down my back, trickling under my stiff collar. I hadn't washed the shirt since I got there and the collar had yellowed in that time. Under the palm trees the cats lay in droves, lethargic and drooling. I took her to the city hall: it's cooler in there, there's an atrium. I ordered iced coffee, can I feel your forehead, she had a cold sweat. Do you feel sick? I'm going to faint, she complained, on the verge of tears. Beneath the thick skin in the rounded transition between thumb and palm, one of her veins pulsed like a worm on a hook.

The coffee was black, a layer of chewy, yellow foam. Lots of sugar please. The ice sounded like rocks on the bottom of the sea when she stirred the drink with her straw. Above us was the echoing sound of footsteps, voices, a door that opened and closed.

She drank fast, she sighed, she caught her breath. A pearl of saliva at the top of her straw. Sun came and went over the smudged glass ceiling as clouds chased by.

A red mark had developed on her shoulder where she'd carried the bag with her towel. She was massaging it. I was aware of the grimy sweat on my face, between my breasts, between my thighs as they chafed against each other. Are you feeling better, I put a hand on her arm, her eyelashes were sticky. Yeah. She sucked the foam. Could I have a cigarette, she said, timidly. No, I said. Changed my mind. Yes.

She tried to light it but didn't know how, the lighter clicked, the flame died, I took it from her—it's kind of broken, I need to get a new one—and as I lit her cigarette I had the exciting feeling of doing something deeply improper. We smoked in silence. We sealed a secret. On the way home I asked her to blow into my face. Her breath was warm and humid and I couldn't smell anything, just the sweet scent of the fruit we'd eaten by the sea.

I WAS COMPELLED to abandon my plan to leave Ermoupoli. Time was listing. I had thought I was at the end of something and now I saw that I'd been at the beginning.

This time it wasn't a decision I made but something I knew instinctively. And as soon as I knew, I could no longer imagine what it had been like not to know. It was like going from seeing the letters of the alphabet as silent cyphers in one moment and hearing them as sounds in the next. I was given a language. I was given a glimpse of forever.

I felt overwhelmed. My blood was rushing and made everything throb. This new certainty changed everything, the whole life I'd lived up until then, every step that had brought me to the line I was about to cross and which would decisively split one world from another.

WHEN WE STEPPED into the foyer of the house, Olga and I, Helena's footsteps came thundering down the interior spiral staircase—why was she upstairs, had she been looking for us? Searching through my stuff?—I panicked, I started ransacking myself to figure out what she might have found that could give me away even though I didn't know what there was to uncover. She was beside herself, she was screaming, she had crazy eyes, she was bright red, her face looked like a tragedy: where have you been, you can't just wander off just like that, I tried to call you, you didn't pick up, I was here all alone. My voice: we were just—when did you get home—, Olga's voice: oh my god calm down, what's your problem. She tossed her bag on the dusty floor. She pushed past Helena into the building. Helena grabbed hold of her neck, held her still, her face was so close to Olga's that she could have kissed her: you can't go somewhere without telling me, it's impossible to trust you, it's impossible to love you when you are like this.

Helena let go of Olga's neck and they walked in opposite directions as if following stage instructions, instantaneously, Olga up the stairs, Helena into her bedroom where she slammed the door and, I heard though it was muffled by the thick walls, screamed. I stood, in shock, in the foyer where the corrugated steel roof clattered loudly from a pair of cats running over it. I didn't want to cross the threshold into the house. I felt like a giant, a gigantic child; I experienced an intense and numbing shame over my frozen state, over the body that grew larger and larger with each moment.

Finally I did move. I shook off my paralyzation. I walked into the house, up the stairs.

OLGA WAS ON THE ROOF. She was scratching at the powdery wash; her fingers were white. I placed a hand on her back, a caress that made her shrink. She hadn't heard me arrive. I got down next to her, she was stiff, arms limp in front of her body. I caressed her head, this soft, heavy head that she soon lay on my shoulder. She'd crossed her wrists in her lap as if they were bound. I saw the clouds come over the mountains. I said nothing. I held her close like a baby.

I couldn't leave. I had to stay, not for Helena, not for my own sake, but for Olga's. This purpose filled me, it washed over me, it opened my heart like a chestnut.

IT WAS HOT everywhere in Europe. The dry grass died and the soil whitened; the air smelled of sand. We lingered in the shady garden in the mornings, we ate olives and slices of melons, we had our phones, our books, and the water bottles perspired through their blue plastic. Helena sucked the olive pits clean before spitting them onto the ground; Olga gnawed their flesh off and placed the mangled remains in a pile on the table; the pile shifted and grew. She was very quiet, I experienced her as more quiet than usual, a silence that was deafening, but sometimes she looked at me, across the table, and I met her gaze. Helena was rambling, talking incessantly, like someone with a bad conscience; it seemed like she wanted to fill the silence so that nobody would look too closely at yesterday, name her outburst and in so doing conjure it up, give it meaning.

The pergola's foliage had dried and rustled ghostlike overhead. It happens every year, Helena noted. Some might say it's insane to even attempt gardening here. But it is what it is, they had a certain sentimental value for her, the naked roots climbing the wooden lattice. She'd had a vision at one point when she had the pergola constructed over the stone table, when she'd planted the wild grapes, big dinners, lanterns in the lush greenery, that sort of thing. Sunlight that sort of sifted through the leaves, but not like this, not through dead leaves, brittle and sharp, more like the light in a beech forest, green and diluted. Oh well. C'est la vie. Apparently the only plants that survived year after year were her fruit trees, and in truth they weren't hers but had been there before she arrived, and she could not fathom what they lived off, pure willpower perhaps, maybe these puny little trees were responsible for sucking the life force out of the soil of the garden and left nothing for the rest to grow from; at the very least they did get fruit every year. It was likely they would keep growing after all of us had died, survive us all. I don't understand any of this, Helena said, I've never had a green thumb. She turned to Olga, right, I've always been hopeless at making things grow, I can't even be trusted with a cactus, her expression was keen as she made this pronouncement, she was absolutely thrilled by her own personality. What's on the agenda for today, it was so hot she could barely think, makes you crazy, once the heat lets up we could go on that excursion, all of us together, we could go to Delos and look at the ruins. She planned to stay around the house today, she didn't feel up for going to the sea even though the breeze out there must be pleasant, but the bus ride was too much, traveling by bus in this heat, it's enough to kill you, the smell of gasoline, the rubber, yesterday she'd felt close to fainting by the time she got home, it just wasn't worth it.

She wanted to give me money: the two of you should go out for lunch, why don't you go to the beach bar, do something fun, me, I'm so boring, all I want to do is rest when it gets this hot. She had the weather report in front of her: twenty-nine degrees, can't be, feels like forty. My brain is on fire. But it takes the biggest toll on the elderly, hopefully they're hydrating. You have to hydrate, she told Olga, otherwise you'll get heatstroke. Put sunscreen on your scalp, too, it's awful to get sunburned there. But the humidity is the worst part, she said, this stuffy feeling, it's like you can't breathe. She sucked on an olive pit, she pulled in her cheeks. She wanted to go lie down in her bedroom, she shook her cigarette pack, could you get me more smokes please, and water.

I hauled the six-packs from the neighborhood grocery store, the big one, six times one and a half liters, we finished them in one day, the empties rolled and banged across the kitchen floor whenever the garden door was open. Salt and water in an ecosystem. The skin grew sticky with sweat followed by a rough dryness. Helena was docile and sweet, she petted Olga's head, she pinched her arm: you should eat more, honey, don't forget that you're still growing. Olga came with me to the store. Olga came with me to the sea. Olga came with me when I left the table, she came with me like a shadow.

WE WENT to the museum that abutted the city hall. One euro to enter, a terrazzo floor in shades of creamed lobster; three rooms packed with graves and offerings to the dead; pigmented seashells. It was cool in there, an even flow of chilled air puffing from the AC system, it gave us goose bumps, the hairs stood up on Olga's arm, her skin was knotted. She studied every object in close detail, the urns and the figurines, the faces in marble; she observed with an excessive attention, almost theatrical. I kept close to her. I looked where she looked. I was attentive to the way she moved, the way her eyes read the words, how her mouth moved almost imperceptibly when she did.

A round mummy portrait from the Roman era hung on the wall beneath one of the tall windows. One hand on the heart, cloth hewn from stone, but the face was gone, chiseled off, a round and violent depression where it should have been. I asked the woman at the ticket counter why it was missing. She said it was impossible to know, it might have been plundered, maybe the face was sold at some point in the past. I wanted to believe that it was a memory that had been excised. I told Olga about this genre of punishment, where the traces of a person's existence were attacked, family portraits with one of the faces erased. I wouldn't care, she said with confidence, I'd be glad to be erased, I wish there were no photos of me.

We stepped into the white light, walking slowly. They'd begun to erect a stage on the square. The world championships were to begin that same day—so we were informed by a drape in sporty design. Olga remembered the sports divers from her childhood, it was special, she was always fascinated by their dress, the diving goggles, a Cyclops eye, she used to think they were superhuman, that they were able to hold their breath indefinitely.

She changed. She got excited talking about herself when I asked questions, my own questions, no longer hers reflected back at her. She stumbled over her words, rushing to get them out. I said: slower. Breathe, you're not underwater. I put a hand on her back. You're really special. You're so intelligent for your age. Your name is beautiful, I've always loved that name. She told me it was from her grandmother, a woman who, people in the family said, had premonitory dreams, dreams that predicted accidents, fires, deaths, never good news. She would like to have dreams like that herself, she would like to know before everyone else did. But she'd never had a dream that came true. She had never met her namesake, who died before Olga was born, "way before," she said, but when I asked she told me a year, not at all that long before Olga was born, seven years earlier, a year that held particular associations for me. I was a child then but old enough to grasp certain things about the world and myself. When I saw photos of myself from that time I could clearly recall what feelings I'd had, I remembered news events from that year and thought of them as part of the contemporary. I realized that the decade must have seemed historic to Olga since she hadn't yet existed. That's how I experienced the time before my own birth, like a story that might be true or untrue, less real but also more significant, more charged, as if everything that happened without me held a different, larger meaning.

She paused in front of the squids on Chiou as if spell-bound. They lay in ice-filled Styrofoam troughs, mottled blisters for heads, slimy tentacles like curly hair. A few were upside down, tentacles folded under the body, splayed like grotesque flowers with pale red suckers. There was a smell of fish in the air, not sharp but fresh like saltwater. The heat had softened the edges of the ice cubes, which were now translucent like rock crystals. Fifteen euros per kilo, she pointed at one, I paid, they gave it to me wrapped in paper and I held it in my arms as we walked to the port, we paused to look at everything, the cats, the canaries outside the pet shop, the garlands of sausage outside the butcher, the jewelry, amber and coral. We walked along the sea, the sailboats, the Nike statue, the sword, the bay leaf wreath, honor and glory, the sun high in the sky. We were quiet and blissful. We were in the midst of something eternal, I could feel it taking shape, time was bending around me to make space for us. The world's beauty flowed through me. I was happy, the richest woman on earth. I was close to a great love.

I SLICED the tentacles apart, holding taut their connecting folds. Olga was with me in the kitchen, she wanted to touch the head, the hole where the beak had been, the plump, shiny flesh. She squealed when it came out, hard and covered with slime; she laughed, she held it between her thumb and index finger.

Helena came out of her tiny bedroom like a ghost or a teenager, she'd just woken up, her eyes were swollen, sheet marks lined her cheek, what are you two doing? She was going for curious; it came out sad. I've been sleeping all day, impossible to get a good rest when it's this hot. Olga fell silent. An octopus, can you imagine. Helena lifted one of the slack tentacles. I'd poured oil into a pot, the oil fizzled and popped, a sound that filled the kitchen. Olga left, went out into the garden, Helena's gaze trailed her. Helena's eyes were a bit sticky; she blinked repeatedly. She told me, voice quiet: now she's upset with me. Did she go out with you today? Did you go to the sea? I can't help that I worry, I didn't know she was with you the other day, she's liable to take off if you don't keep an eye on her, I thought it would be different here where she doesn't know anybody. She lit a cigarette. I held the tentacles over the oil, dropped them in one by one. They curled up like snails. But with you it's different, she said, I can trust you.

IN THE EVENING she let Olga have a small glass of wine. She made a big deal out of it, you're old enough, just this small glass won't hurt, but not more than a tiny bit, I don't want you to think it's a regular event, it's only because I'm being extra nice that you're allowed to drink tonight. The octopus suckers were dark red and hardened; the whirring of the cicadas and the humming of the mopeds came through the dark. We lit the lanterns and Olga didn't leave. Helena waxed melancholic, she wanted to talk about her dad. I'm bad at grief, she said, it's heavy, aging, death is heavy. She sounded like she was reading from a pamphlet. I looked at Olga, her dark eyes, her hand clutching the short stem of the wineglass as if she were guarding it, her lower lip moist from licking, a halfmoon mark on the cup. Summer, it doesn't go with death, or I guess it goes with everything. Helena was speaking as if we weren't there, sounding simultaneously as if she were talking to herself and as if she were holding forth before a large audience; it was a lonely way of talking. It's a horrid thought, grass growing over him in the memorial grove. She would have preferred a headstone for her dad, for herself, a monument to visit. But of course we'll all be overgrown, she said, everywhere we've walked the grass will grow, grass wins in the end, and nevertheless I, personally, can't ever make anything grow, isn't that ironic—she was slurring a little— ishn't that ironic. How little remains. Olga took a big drink of wine. Her throat expanded, a sound like a cartoon character: cluck.

I saw Helena glance at Olga and there was something

I didn't understand in that look. It was critical, mournful, loving; it made me feel very alone where I was sitting across the table, watching them, my cheeks a little stiff, my jaw, the corners of my mouth, skin crawly, a sense of impatience. Teetering between smile and grin. That glance, it put me on the defensive, or maybe I was ready to pounce, I could rarely tell which was which. Shame the predominant feeling, but there was a strong sense of having the upper hand too: I saw them, I saw it all.

Something changed in Helena's face and I worried that her pensiveness would flip again, turn into anger. But it wasn't anger, it was excitement, suddenly she was all enthusiasm: the bronze horse in the archaeological museum in Athens, had she told us already, did she tell us about the towing of the bronze horse? I really should take the time to go. It was a diver who found it, Helena said, not even a hundred years ago, they were diving for sponges, they thought it was a ship-wreck full of corpses, human bodies, horses on the bottom of the sea. Imagine a diver's suit from that time, a morbid image that made her tremble with pleasure: the heavy mask, the glass, the darkness, picture that! But it wasn't corpses they saw, the ship had been there since antiquity, loaded with statues.

Olga licked her middle finger and started running it along the edge of the wineglass. It didn't make a sound. I watched her do it, watched the lantern reflected in the glass, how it was briefly blocked from view each time she completed a circle with her finger, it blinked like a lighthouse.

I smiled at her with my rigid face. She lifted her gaze. She smiled at me.

Just think, that this is when we are alive. What a coincidence to be living right now, that we came to be born after the towing of the statues, that we have the chance to see something so many others could never see, these objects, they were on the bottom of the sea for several thousands of years. Such a small wonder of time. She misspoke; she meant a small window of time. On the other hand it would have been beautiful if they'd been allowed to remain in the depths, until the end of time. Imagine, she said, when you toss a pebble into the ocean, you might be the last person ever to touch that stone. Of course it doesn't hold any meaning when you really think about it, but still, isn't it . . . it could have been beautiful, if they'd let them stay, buried down there. But perhaps all graves are robbed in the end. That's what's nice about ashes, and what's sad about them too, you erase everything, you leave no trace.

IN THE MORNING it rained twice. Short, warm downpours that had no effect on the heat or humidity and which left the air smelling of clay and bay leaves, the sun crashing down. The yard's white soil turned into a sludge that dried into a hard crust, only to soften again. Fruits came hurling from the branches. Helena wanted to do nothing. Helena wanted silence.

Olga and I went to the docks in the afternoon. They were teeming with people, the beach bar was packed, the air was still, the sea was clucking and babbling, the concrete coarse against the skin.

Olga gazed covetously at the horizon, the boats. How come you never swim? She said she didn't want to get salt in her eyes. You could just close your eyes, you don't have to put your head under. But I want to put my head under, she said, it's not the same if you don't. I'm not going to do it just because you're pestering me about it. She grew sulky. I regretted having said anything. I wanted her forgiveness: as you wish. I got up and the heat rose through my body, up my legs, it went to my head, it blurred my vision, I walked away from her, dove in from the edge, the sound was like a gunshot. Something clicked and shut around my eardrums. I heard the muted roaring of the sea, felt the chill over my eyelids, my hair trailing me like a tail, and then something grabbed hold of me and I kicked, I took a breath before I had broken the surface, water burned in my nose and throat. She had followed me. She was treading water, sinking a little, she couldn't reach the bottom, she tilted her head back, mouth open. I laughed at her.

The dock after. Her thigh beside mine, close, a cold insinuation, the goose bumps, saltwater. Not too close. We drank our water, now lukewarm, it tasted like plastic. She held her bottle in both hands as she drank. The sun was dipping behind the dome, people started to leave, she asked me if she could swim again and it excited me that she sought my permission, I told her you're allowed to do exactly what you want. Do what I want. She went in on the ladder, she held on, her head glittered. She glided out. Her body a cross, still, like a piece of paper. I saw her cheeks and nose rise out of the water, her closed-eyed marble face.

ON THE ROOF I asked if I could take her picture: you're so beautiful. The sun gilded the pale hairs on her back, they looked like someone had combed them into a curl, they were so delicate against her tanned back, like threads of silk. Her earphones leaked; the music sounded like someone breathing. When she rolled onto her back the wires climbed over her breasts like white nerves.

She said no. She didn't like being photographed. When she closed her eyes I almost did it anyway. Maybe she could sense me, my shadow over her body, but she didn't open her eyes. She would have let me. I wanted to preserve everything, the shoulders, the sun-warm skin, I wanted to fix her face in time. When she closed her eyes I observed her uninterrupted, hungrily, her shallow belly button, the skin that was darker over her eyes and between her legs, the bikini, the mound of her crotch. I didn't take a photo. I didn't want to ruin the memory.

I lay down. I stretched out. I closed my eyes against the light. Through my eyelids I could sense her movement, her mass next to mine, her shadow, the darkness then the sharp light, my veins like tiny, bright brooks. Heart beating against the ground. We lay like that for a long time, side by side in the afternoon sun.

I put out my arm for her to rest her head on. Her irises labored under the eyelids, back and forth like she was dreaming. The corners of her mouth like where the stalk had been plucked on a peach. I rubbed her back, long scratches, my arm around her like a claw, my leg between hers. She said harder, then slower. More. She smiled and the corners of her mouth clicked.

Her pleasure was so pure. I used to love this when I was small, she said, Mom would always scratch my back when I couldn't fall asleep . . . I pictured her a girl, belly down, back tanned, white panties, nail marks on the flesh. I stopped, aghast. She opened her eyes: don't stop!

I continued. Slower, harder. She closed her eyes again. Her eyelids a little glossy from grease or sweat. Her lips faintly separated. She shivered, her thighs tensed, bumpy like after the swim even though she was warm. You're so beautiful. Did I tell you that? Really special. On the roof we were close to heaven and close to the precipice, far from the world but near ourselves, in our own time, our own room.

I STARTED TO THINK it had been some kind of desire, still unknown to me at the time, that brought me to Ermoupoli. I thought it was about one thing: my need for validation, my desire for Helena's acceptance, her love, my desire to become an indispensable, fixed part of her interior life. The idea of the city's beauty appealed to me. The name appealed to me. Now I was thinking instead that the enigmatic allure of the place had always been rooted in something else, dictated not by my own consciousness and dreams but, rather, by fate. It was an intoxicating thought. That there was meaning. That my life had a direction of its own. That I too was a participant in a world I usually felt like I was observing from the outside.

HELENA WANTED TO GO to the square to watch the world championships. Yeah, they've been going on for three days. I told her what we'd seen when we left the dock that afternoon, a stage, big crowds, Helena wanted to go and be part of that crowd, why didn't you say anything—a quality like anger in her voice, it was sharp, hard, you idiot. I savored this anger because it was an intimate anger, the type of anger expressed between members of a family.

Now she wanted to have dinner at the square and I regretted having said anything. I was of two minds, going with her would mean leaving Olga home alone like that evening at Oneiro. But Olga wanted to come, yeah I guess I can come, her voice quiet, timid, polite. Cautious, why not, whatever, and I saw how happy it made Helena, she was surprised and happy to hear it, borderline euphoric. Suddenly she was champing at the bit to leave, as if we had to hurry before Olga changed her mind. For the first time since my arrival to the island she put on perfume. We walked there and when the sidewalk narrowed I ended up behind them, too far back to catch more than fragments of their conversation but close enough to smell the scent that trailed Helena. The scent, her perfume, pitched me straight into a state that already seemed passé, part of an older life. It made me nostalgic to remember it. Their closeness made me sad, the way they constantly found their way back to their places, how they returned to each other.

The curtains hung like ghosts in the windows of the city hall. The palm trees were illuminated by bright lights, and the facade, I'd never seen the square in the dark before. Around the streetlights the sky was low, dirty, the cosmos far away; there were no stars between the arches. The pigeons were there and the marble stones gleamed; sounds were coming from the stage. I was seated between Olga and Helena like a borderline or a hyphen. Helena focused on the images on the screen. She spoke in half-sentences, she was distracted by the surroundings, she was commenting on the things we saw, she wanted grilled fish, it wasn't on the menu but she was sure, 100 percent sure, that she'd smelled it from another table, she made a complex order. White wine in a carafe, soda for Olga, a bottle of Coca-Cola and a tall glass with lemon slices and ice. Olga shrank, became small at the table. Her posture was bad. Her shoulders sloped forward, she drank from the straw without picking up the glass. The gray sea on the screen was illuminated; it turned blue. Helena's small movements, an unremitting tension in her shoulders, her jaw, she couldn't tear her gaze from the distance, the luster over there, the men, their hats, the teenage boys.

The pigeons took off from the square in a flapping cloud, their wings beating like a rain. The teens were chasing them with wild faces that straightened out when the birds lifted. It seemed like they understood that what they were doing was childish, a game they had outgrown that should no longer give them joy. They were testing the boundaries of childhood, or adulthood maybe, chasing pigeons ironically, self-consciously, without genuine excitement and desire, but nonetheless they repeated their choreography again and again, their attack on the pigeons as soon as they landed. It was aggressive. It was just a game.

The three of us watched the square and the stage in silence. But now and then I noticed how Olga seemed to seek my gaze, quiet but intent, as if waiting for a cue that never came. It silenced me, sitting between her and Helena; I felt I couldn't talk to Olga in front of Helena and that feeling egged me on, we were hiding something together. The wine was sweet and we smoked over the plates and the glasses on the table; the carafe was greasy with fingerprints and onstage they weighed the fish as voices thundered through the microphone, bounced off arches, stone walls, the old buildings that encircled us and the crowd. A wind came in from the sea, up the street, past the Nike statue, honor and victory, and from the port came the sound of the ferry and its farewell melody that by now had been etched in me, stubborn and ridiculous on top of the brooding horn.

I met Olga's gaze. I returned my attention to the square.

I looked at the teenagers and the lives they held in front of them, looked at this memory they would keep or lose, the flight of the pigeons, the palm trees and the scent of frying oil, coconut, plastic, and sand that stuck to bodies and clothes. The last childhood games, the puny hair under arms and between legs, the sweat that had started to smell, semen at night. It looked like they were hiding in their clothes, their thick sweaters like turtle shells, sleeves pulled down, collars popped so half their faces were covered; their legs were so thin and naked, their knees like foals', feet large, bodies out of tune.

It didn't occur to me then that they might have been Olga's age. You can't know with boys; they might have been older, they seemed younger, much younger. They were their own species. They followed their own logic. It was impossible for me to think of her as one of them.

We ordered yet another carafe of wine, yet another soda in a glass bottle, more ice. We didn't move when the crowd thinned and the boys reunited with their fathers, and soon the restaurants too emptied, quieted. It's how I would remember it, as if the sounds around us gradually evaporated while the silence between the three of us held, and we sat where we were even as they cleared out the tables, the amps, and the winners' stand until all that was left was the scaffolding, bare and mute in the darkness, like a ruin.

WE WALKED up the stairs past the tourism agency and the ferry-ticketing office, past the casino, the chapel, the store that sold musical instruments. The lights were on at a patio where two old women were seated with a boy. He looked odd. Protruding eyes, head like an egg, he looked like a painting by Goya. For a moment, as we approached this trio, which, in a strange way, resembled ours, I wondered if I was imagining the scene. The women were dressed in black, they were smoking, they flanked the boy on either side and the way they sat together made it seem like they were guarding him or perhaps watching over him. There was something dreamlike and ancient about them, solemn and altar-like, the impression punctured only by certain objects around them: plastic planters, the sound of a TV or radio leaking through the half-open terrace door; these objects anchored them in the world I inhabited coming up the stairs. Helena said hello when we passed; the women nodded at her, said hello back, the boy sat between them silent and inert, his gaze fixed exactly where it had been the whole time we walked toward and then past them.

I felt a pang of discomfort and pity as we passed, the absolute loneliness of that body, the stillness of his eyes; it pained and scared me as we continued on, Helena and Olga ahead and me just behind them, right there, silent. It all seemed so distant in the night. The sun was distant and the white roof, the head on the arm, my leg between the thighs distant, even though that same person was walking right in front of me. It was impossible. It couldn't be the same person, could not be the person who was presently walking arm in arm with her mother.

When I flipped the light switch in the foyer we were blinded, the light was white and glossy, almost green. The night seemed to have deepened Helena's wrinkles and her face was shiny; she brought her hands to her head and moved them through her hair like a prayer, she was dead tired, she gave Olga a hug, I'd never seen her do that before, I smelled the familiar mix of sweat and perfume.

The embrace bothered me. It was a small foyer and I felt in the way, too close, too much a participant and too much an outsider, a jealous witness. I felt impatient, on the brink of something big; I felt pregnant with it. I was anxious about the night, which would become day.

I remained where I stood as Helena moved deeper inside the house. I watched her very tired gait, her defeated steps.

OLGA AND I brushed our teeth in front of the bathroom mirror. It was she who followed me once Helena had gone inside, lain down, crashed. I made space for her next to me at the sink, a familiar gesture I associated with my previous romantic relationships, a life lived side by side, the space you make for the other and the space they make for you when you reach for something, pass each other, spit past each other; it was an unfamiliar gesture because it was her and I'd never been so close to her in the night. I watched her in the mirror and her reflection gazed back, the black eyes, the woolly eyebrows, the wide mouth full of foam. She brushed hard so I brushed harder, until the toothbrush hit my soft insides, jaw tense and rigid.

I was fatigued. I felt desire make its return from the day. More palpable now, purer, stronger and more dangerous, no longer dismissible; it was no longer possible to conceive of not acting on it. I saw a possibility. But I had to be cautious. I sensed the ecstatic feeling of anticipation, the certainty and hesitation of my movements; I sensed my toeing the line. Close to the underworld. I reined in my movements, made them smaller, slower.

Olga spat, a string of blood in the foam. I spat. The light in the bathroom whirred and quivered and made it look like she was trembling as she turned the faucet and everything drained in a gurgling spiral.

We merged in the mirror. When I looked at her it was as if I saw myself. When I kissed her I liberated her from something: her childhood, her mother.

THERE WAS NO TALKING that night. I listened to her breath, I followed it, I followed the sound when she swallowed. I listened for the line between fear and desire. I was very slow. Very mild. She: stiff at first, still, then soft. A look of overwhelming imploration, almost fright.

That face made me crazy afterward. It came back to me and I didn't even need to conjure it; I fell, headless. It made me feel powerful. I had given her this face. I had created this uninhibited face, one I was convinced would be with her for the rest of her life.

TWO TERRIBLE DAYS split by a terrible, lonely night followed. I lay awake for hours, waiting; we didn't talk in the daytime and the humidity and the low skies were worse than ever, none of us left the house. Helena wanted ice-cold water upon waking, coffee, an orange she peeled very slowly in tiny increments, and all we could manage for dinner was bread and olives; it was as though we'd all been consumed by illness.

Olga looked different. She was no longer the same person. My memories became hazy and violent and I was not doing well. I was unsure of what had happened and the only way I could check was by playing the same mental images again and again until they no longer seemed real. I turned inward. Talking to Helena my voice sounded weirdly sludgy, like a recording in slow motion.

I picked a pomegranate and peeled it for dinner. One of the chambers was full of rotten seeds—just one of them, brown, sticky, a sick section in the otherwise-healthy fruit. There was no transition, only a boundary where the seeds on one side were red and bright, and ruined on the other. A deformity. I tossed the whole fruit; I didn't want to touch anything that had touched the rot, grown inside the same casing.

But the second night I lay awake in bed, unable to sleep again, there was rain, then thunder. It came out of the darkness, the cats screamed and took shelter. It made the window's wooden hatches rattle. It brought with it a scent of seaweed and salt from the sea, sand and dust from the streets, it drenched the towel I'd left hanging over the balcony railing, it pulled cold air and noise into my room. I saw a flash, like a wink, and started to count until the rolling thunder. It wasn't far away. The sound was so powerful that it seemed like the storm might tear the house from its foundations, the sound alone, shatter all this stone, this city, let it float off and sink into the sea. An island is exposed. I imagined the coastline, the hillside, the stones of the beaches and the dry, pitched slopes, the pine groves and the docks, everything coming down, crashing.

There was another lightning strike, soundless. The slash of light. Then the crash. Rain beat the steel roof; the weights on the mosquito netting rattled. Shipwreck.

Olga came to my room. She came back to me. I didn't see her until she was right next to me, by the bed, she wore her sheet like a cape, I couldn't sleep. I said: come here. I took her hand. She didn't resist. Let's count, I said. One one thousand. Two one thousand. The thunder was coming closer. The lightning made the night look like something else, a strobe light, a dream as we lay next to each other, gazing out.

Did the storm scare her? Was she not too old to be scared of thunder? Would she have sought comfort elsewhere if I hadn't been there, would she have sought it from her mother?

I pressed her hand and she held on harder when the room lit up, the storm was right above us, it was so exciting, I could've screamed. Instead I just held her harder. I held on to her like a splinter from a wreckage. We waited out the storm. We counted the distance between light and sound. It grew bigger and bigger, seven one thousand, eight one thousand, as the rain kept rushing down and washing everything away, leaving nothing as it tore through.

She squeezed my hand. She came to me. She had nowhere else to go. I became her mother that night, I rocked her, I nursed her.

5.

❧ Bilitis ❧

TIME TOOK ON A DIFFERENT MEANING. The days came with a new sort of loneliness, the loneliness of being with others, the loneliness of the other: across from Olga at the table, the coffee, the flies. She stopped taking sugar. Half milk. Her bitter tongue.

Helena announced that she had started to work on something. It was after the storm, it was the scents whipped up by the rain, it was the tension that let go, finally you can breathe again, finally you can be outdoors, she wanted to take long walks, she wanted to pull the air deep down into her lungs. She hadn't heard the thunder at all but she'd felt it in her bones; it had found its way into her dreams.

The darkness grew sharper, the air was more crisp.

Helena showed us pictures she'd taken, natural scenes outside the city, terraced gardens, wild grass, basically barren landscapes. The city was lush in comparison, its gardens, the bougainvillea covering the alleyways, the pine groves on the hills abutting the sea, the palm trees, the shoots poking out between rocks, fig leaves. The colors were sharper now. The world contained enormous beauty. A pleasure lingered in the fingers, the tongue.

The loneliness of the evening: Olga who left, the glowing window. It was behind Helena's back, out of her sightline, a promise. Helena was in the way, she was between us like a guard dog ignorant of its role. The late evenings alone with her became long and drawn out, no longer the thing I looked forward to and then missed when they ended. I felt hopeless when she stood up to get another bottle of wine, or whenever she thought of something just as some topic had started to run its course and launched into the new story with renewed enthusiasm.

Helena spent her days going on long excursions, today I saw all the way to Gyaros. Helena brought her camera, Helena made observations in her notebook, today it was like I'd regained my sight—she hadn't felt this full of vitality in a long while, not since before moving to Sweden, the cumbersome demands of daily life; once again she had the sense of being part of the world. She fell asleep on the rocky beach and dreamed short, terrible dreams; she almost had sleep paralysis. She had dreams where she was buried alive. She had dreams of statues screaming in horror, she had dreams of vaults splintering and crashing, dreams of fire, falling meteorites, thick clouds of smoke, subterranean rivers. But she wasn't scared, it was so beautiful all of it, she always knew she was dreaming but she couldn't make it stop. It was so beautiful, she said, it was like the last judgment.

I was an attentive rock. I looked toward the glow.

Next, the wait, in the bedroom, under the covers, door open to the sea, door open to the landing. Listening to the sounds that linked me with the rest of the world: the ferry's horn and the booming of the sea, civilization and nature. Listening to the sounds that anchored me and tied me down: the creaking of the floor molding, the feet, the door that Olga shut behind her.

When she caressed my face the sound was a storm. Pale fire beneath the skin. We have to be quiet. Listening to the muted hhh of our breathing, the sound of our bodies, the whooshing sea in our ears as if her hands were seashells.

The rest of time was without meaning. The rest of time was waiting, misgivings, forgetting. The dizzying feeling of remembering who she was, to remember, in daylight, the distance. To reject the thought of her childhood. At night she came loose from her age and so did I; I left my chronology behind and found a new order of time, a chronology of love. Without past, without grief. Without future too.

A hand over her mouth, the heat and the humidity, her sucking inhalation, those were the sounds that linked me to forever.

I FANTASIZED about a particular picture, a photograph. I wouldn't have been able to take it myself and she wouldn't have been able to either. We would have needed a third person. Somebody who wanted us to be beautiful. Somebody who wanted to preserve this image: the image of our bodies lying next to each other, one bigger and one smaller, one pale and one dark, like a shadow cleft in two.

THE TEENS TOUCHED each other's hair under the parasol, they put their heads in each other's laps, cheek against groin. Not too intimate. I never touched Olga by the sea, only in ways that would look unintentional. I brushed against her neck: there's a mosquito there, let me help you with the sunscreen. When we were in the water together, when I put my head under, I found pleasure in the irregular slapping sounds in the water, which I took to be Olga's body nearby. I saw her long arms stretch out in the water, her body shortened under the surface, legs white, pale blue. When we walked back, the square, the stairs, I held her arm in mine. Two women, nothing to it. Two sisters, two friends, a mother and her daughter.

Olga had a dignified expression. Olga grew tall next to me when I held her.

Occasionally she swatted off my hand the way she would have bat at her mother's hand, a swift and familiar gesture; humiliating, crushing. The arm she disentangled when we approached the house, the posture: slouching, she walked a couple of steps ahead of me, she left me. The cherished solitude of the afternoons when we slowly dried off on the roof, before the evening, before Helena returned. A hand on a thigh. We were visible to everyone and no one, out of reach under the sun, attentive to the sounds that marked the end: footsteps on Persefonis, the hollow rattling of the door to the house.

Fear and desire side by side, inseparable like a double helix. It sings in the veins, it twists. It would be easy to confuse one with the other, you could spend your whole life doing it unless you were careful. It wasn't unpleasant. The sounds on Chiou became louder: the canaries in their cages, the music. The smells from the fishmonger became sharp and pungent, the smells from the butcher became thick and bloody, the meat looked grotesque on the hooks, the slabs, red and splayed, white, thick fat like intarsia. The eyes of strangers. A sharp anxiety in Helena's voice, I never knew if it was actually there or if I was projecting my own feelings, when I came down the stairs, when she came through the door: where have you—did you just get here—is Olga—, she often appeared surprised to see me and also impatient, annoyed. Yeah, we went to the sea, she's in her room, I don't know, it really was nice today, quite windy . . . a look of relief tinged with disappointment: how nice for you both. It's kind of you to take her out.

Part of me never wanted to be without it, never wanted to be without the fear of being found out, never wanted to be liberated from the intense presence that resulted from listening, weighing the distance. Wait.

Our whispers in the night: this is absolutely secret. What we are doing is very risky. But she did it, she crossed the landing, night after night. She crossed the line into my room. Nobody had ever done anything like that for me before.

It feels like a book, Olga said with her long beautiful o, a book, a bouk. Olga's entire emotional life was built from the shadows of things she'd read. She measured her world with books, not the other way around. This was how she rediscovered things she'd only ever had described to her. The feeling of infatuation. The feeling of desire. It was just like a book. So what I gave her with my hands and mouth was life itself.

IN OLGA'S ROOM back in Atlas, one day when my desire to get a glimpse had grown too strong—not a desire for her, to learn something about her, since at that point she held no interest to me, but a desire to learn more about Helena, to procure a better hand than she could know I had, to truly get to know her and not just the version of her that she'd presented to me—I saw a hairbrush, covered in thick, dark wool. Later, this detail was all I could recall about this room. When I tried to remember what it looked like, the image I pictured was identical to Olga's room in Ermoupoli, equally small and bare, impersonal, cloister-like. I never crossed the threshold. I shut the door as soon as I'd opened it, fast, before Helena, who was taking one of her many long baths, would come and find me.

But the brush, it seared itself into my mind. Maybe because it repulsed me, that mat of lost hair. Maybe because it looked expensive: heavy, ivory-white. I started to think of it as a sign. I wanted to collect all the banal details, create a line of love; I was obsessed with knowing. I wanted to hear her say: this whole time I was thinking of you, longing for you, I wanted to be where you were. Say it again. Tell me again. That first time when you saw me, what do you remember. I lied to her, I said: I could tell right then, I knew immediately, this is the great love, this is . . . I could no longer remember anything outside of this story; everything was a premonition when I looked back.

The brush, I never told her about it, but I came to think of it as our first encounter, the first hint of a crush. This trace of her previous life, one where she'd had long hair she would brush, mommy's girl, the life she'd already left but of which, on the threshold to her room, I had caught a glimpse.

I fantasized about how she'd imagined me before we met, just as I'd imagined her. I fantasized about what kinds of feelings my name had inspired in her. I said: I can't believe that I knew about you for so long, almost a year, without knowing anything, without realizing what was waiting for me.

I asked what she knew about me before I came to Ermoupoli. Nothing, she said.

Nothing? But you must have known something. Who did your mom say was coming? Some person, she replied.

She fell asleep before me that night, eyelashes dark and spiky against her cheek, mouth slightly open, shiny red line inside the lips.

ASTERIA'S BAR HAD ENDED their service for the season. The cafés and restaurants in the port were closing, the sailboats no longer set anchor, the sidewalk tables that remained were increasingly unoccupied. Night came earlier than before and motor sounds moved through the darkness at night. The dock in Vaporia was now in the shade and we went to the one farther away, below the shuttered bar, the tall wall with cacti. The wooden deck behind the dock had an unpleasant smell, bodily, like stale alcohol; we sat there and watched the waves come in one straight line, headed toward the green cliffs, the stones below the dock: you had to climb the ladder to get in, you couldn't jump from there, it might kill you. Foam bloomed against the concrete and the music from the retirees on the first dock reached all the way to us; from where we sat I spotted the man with the bandage, still green, his healthy foot in the water, his eyes on the horizon. He seemed at once very childish and very old, hunched over, his body's small size and incongruous dexterity, his face sad like a silent movie.

It was Olga's idea to go to the sea. An alibi? I could've stayed inside forever with her. I would've closed the door, lowered the blinds, shut her in, created a place where we were free and unseen. But she was in charge, she was the one wielding her power over me.

And I loved walking to the sea with her, side by side, being in the world with her, being part of it. Squinting in the relentless light. Passing the souvenir shop with the shells, Blanc du Nil with the white clothes. One time, in the silence that settled between us there, in our steps on the stones, I caught a glimpse of a different life, as if through a door cracked open. Maybe that life was happening somewhere else; maybe this life could have been possible, one where she and I had always known each other, seen everything together, where we would continue to do so. I fantasized about being part of her family, but I knew families weren't like that. You don't see the same things. You have your own history. You can't escape the voice telling the story.

I noticed what was inside Olga's movements. I paid attention to the person she was about to become, a person I suspected—knew—I would never meet. Someone else was waiting in the wings. Someone else would burst out of her. She would become a different person. She would become herself. She would become the person I had now participated in creating, through my life intersecting with hers.

Her breathless words at night: I'm so glad I met you.

She'd been on earth for such a short time and she didn't know it; she'd been on earth her entire life, for that whole long childhood she was so impatient to leave behind. She moved as if her limbs annoyed her, as if she wanted to get rid of them. I thought about her teens, this time of her life I was witnessing. I thought about the other life. It was no less real than the other lives I could sense as we walked down the city's streets, across the square, down the stairs, and toward the sea, the lives that were over, the lives currently happening, the lives still in the future. All of them possibilities. They held many promises, grief and happiness. And I knew so little about them; I knew nothing.

THE TOMB OF BILITIS, on Cyprus. I came to think of this story, this scam, when we were on the dock. I told it to her, using a voice I thought sounded very old when I heard myself. The Cypriotic tomb of Bilitis contained perfume bottles, their scent intact. A silver mirror. A small nude statue of Astarte that kept watch over the poet's skeleton, decorated with gold, snow-white and so fragile it would turn to dust the moment it was touched by breath. I savored the experience of teaching her something, a part of our history.

Imagine a perfume that still smells, long after death, for millennia. Imagine being buried with a goddess. Lilies and corpses share an odor molecule, I've forgotten the name of it. Rotten, rancid. Some people can't stand the smell of lilies; maybe it's because they unconsciously understand their link to death. Olga liked lilies, she told me. She liked their smell. She liked the heft of the bell-like petals, their pollen, the bright red.

What's Astarte? She's a fertility goddess. Goddess of love, goddess of sex, goddess of war. A book by Karin Boye. Karin Boye took her own life, Olga said, oddly solemn, as if she had been personally tasked with delivering the news of death. Yes. Too many suicides in our history. Too many sad women. Too many close friends.

But there was something else I remembered, too, a series of photographs I'd seen a long time ago, taken by a Norwegian woman around the turn of the century and discovered after her death. They were formal studio portraits of her and her lover, dressed as a vestal, indoors, in a boat, accompanied by a dog. Something about the photographer reminded me of Olga. Her short hair, the face, which looked so youthful in the photo, smooth skin, dark, piercing eyes. I couldn't remember her name. It seemed like she'd been happy.

The Songs of Bilitis, I hadn't thought of them in many years, not since my search for pleasure was the same as my search for myself. I was very young then. I was much older than Olga was now.

The author changed the *i* in his surname into a *y*, an i-grec. Pierre Louÿs, an odd name, a name that wouldn't fool anyone. *Y*, in honor of his love for antiquity. I said: that's a book I read, it was a long time ago at this point. Lesbian history. Published in the nineteenth century, a fictional poet. There was never a tomb. No mirror. No perfumes. All of this happened when this city was new, it's all the same aesthetics, the book's illustrations, the women, the folds of their clothes, the curls, the wrists. The Swedish title: *Female Friends: Bilitis's Songs About Love*. Always these female friends. One of the songs: I shall take your mouth into my mouth as the child takes its mother's breast. Yikes.

You should read it sometime, I said, and melancholia washed over me. Her future was in that sentence, the future beyond this island, the future beyond this borrowed time. I saw a band extend into the future, all her summers, the summers that would come after this, the summer she would come back here. Not me.

She got up to swim and I stayed behind with my melancholia, my rage.

A MAN MY AGE was harvesting sea urchins with a tong. He was wearing goggles and swim trunks with long legs that ballooned in the water. When he surfaced for air his dark hair lay slicked to his forehead and then he dove again, he hewed close to the rocks near the dock, it looked dangerous. There was the sound of gulls, of ducks, the ferry passing, Olga: it's sounding its horn at the church, it's bad luck not to do it. Do you believe in God? I told her no. Olga said she did believe in God since she never felt alone, since she always felt that someone was watching over her. It made me jealous. I wanted to be mean to her.

She got in the water using the ladder, she swam out, far. I sat on the dock. The man who was harvesting sea urchins resembled a dog splashing in the water, the repeated dives, the open mouth when he surfaced. He kept his catch in a mesh tote. He came up the ladder with the tote in one hand, his body pudgy, unevenly tanned: white belly, white thighs where his swim trunks had ridden up.

Olga swam to the ladder. Olga came to sit by my side. I crossed one leg over the other; she sat with hers open.

The man opened the urchins with scissors, it was violent, water pouring out, a terrible sound: hard, clicking, like cutting through patent leather. His knuckles whitened. I asked if he was selling and he gave us one he'd already opened, we ate it with our fingers, grainy red flesh, I held the spiky shape in my cupped hand for her, careful don't hurt yourself, she dug, she licked under the nails.

The man joined us. He had lemons. He had beer in a plastic

bag full of seawater. He had a motorbike, he explained, it was parked by the church; he'd come to town for groceries but he was camping on the other side of the island, and he told us: you should come to the campsite, you can take a bus. He looked at Olga as he talked. He had no knife for the lemons, he opened them with his scissors, legs spread, he penetrated the peel with the dull blade. He loved the sea, I love the sea, he told us, in English. He slept right by the water's edge. You get a magical sunset over there, nothing like the sun when it sets over the sea. He loved riding his motorbike, adored the speed, the heft of the machine. He'd traveled all the way from the Netherlands. He'd traversed Germany, Austria, Slovenia, Croatia, Bosnia, Albania—and one country he was forgetting, he labored to remember it while Olga and I sat in silence—Montenegro, right before Albania, then on to Greece, where he was now traveling from island to island, the ferries make it easy, there's so much to see in Europe. He looked at Olga's thighs. He looked at Olga's breasts, her stomach. Your hair, he said, it's different, very unusual, it suits you. His accent was slick, oily. Olga's perfect, crystalline, reverberating: does it never get lonely? She sounded so sincere. Politely interested, curious, girlish. By her side I felt my entire body get stiff and silent, a paralyzing anger before her beautiful voice.

The man squeezed the massacred lemon over one of the sea urchins and sucked its contents. Did we have a cigarette he could bum? I gave him my pack. He slipped one out and offered Olga. I took the pack back: she doesn't smoke. She sent me a quick, disappointed glance. No, he explained, he never got lonely. He felt free. He loved the feeling of freedom.

The goggles' rubber seals had left red marks around his eyes that made it look like he'd been crying.

You meet lots of interesting people. He enunciated each syllable like he was singing, in te re sting. He said: I'm a bit of a nomad. I despised him. You can sleep anywhere, he told Olga; listen to the city waking up in the morning, you should try it. I said: no, we can't, it's different for women. My rebuke was annoying.

I was heavy and humorless. I saw Olga's body in between the man's and mine, her smooth arms, the flabbiness of ours. His revolting mouth, thick, wet lips.

I told Olga, in Swedish: it's getting late. He asked what language we were speaking and I pretended not to hear him. When I stood up and buttoned my shirt something about the situation reminded me of a postcoital atmosphere. Come to the campsite later, he said, you know where it is, where to find me. Maybe we'll meet again. Yeah, definitely. He hadn't said his name and I hadn't said mine. As we left, walking to the first dock, toward the music and the stairs, I pictured him stretching his fat white thighs on the warm stone, which was still moist where Olga had been sitting.

How old do you think he thought I was, she asked coquettishly. Twelve, I said. You really think so. Yes, I think he was a pedophile. No, I'm just pulling your leg. I have no clue. She laughed uncertainly. I think he thought I was older, she said with pride. Then, halfway up the stairs: what a boring guy. A glance at me. You think so, I replied, I thought he seemed nice.

We walked in silence past the cathedral, across the square, down to the port. I clutched the strap of my bag slung across my shoulder with both hands as if carrying a cross. I wanted to say: did you see the way he looked at you, but that was something a man would have said, a jealous man, and I was not a man, and I was not jealous.

THAT NIGHT I drank heavily, I stayed late with Helena in the garden, I heard my own voice recede from me, I saw the garden get smaller and smaller, the night closed in on us like a cocoon, and finally I saw the light in the window behind Helena turn off, bottomless agony in the corner of my eye. We put lots of ice in the wine; it had been left on the counter all day. There was water in the center of the ice cubes, Helena complained that the freezer wasn't really doing its job, nothing froze completely in just one day, it didn't get through to the center. But both night and day were cooler, not like before. Helena, with a look of authority: this is the shift, fall is coming to the Aegean Sea; she said it like an oracle, she loved saying "the Aegean Sea," how sumptuous and bright, how frightening that these very waves were lapping the beaches of Gyaros too, turquoise and crystalline, like in paradise.

Her face had calcified in the sun, dried and stiffened. Makes you tired, she said, to sit here night after night, don't you think—when did you get here anyway, it feels like forever ago at this point. She let her gaze linger on me and attempted to clasp her hands on the table but missed and settled for closing one open hand around the other fist.

For a brief moment I thought I would tell her. I wouldn't, never, I would deny every accusation if I had to, and I found myself bowled over by the force of this never. Up until this moment I'd never even imagined the possibility, this parallel story where I could harm her in a real way, where I could harm myself. I had something to tell, something that concerned her, something that would cause me to haunt her, and, I realized right then, something that would alienate me from her forever. The danger made me feel like I was breathing water. My face was warm and I put a cool hand to it, touching my ear, the gesture that exposes a liar.

Yeah definitely, it does make you tired, but rested too, but yeah the sun makes you tired, it's quite something, when did I get here?—it does feel like long ago, I agree.

I understood from her question that I had stayed too long and this fact no longer concerned me. I missed it, the time, technically speaking not at all long ago, when those words, said in the same way, would absolutely have crushed me.

We finished the bottle. We listened to the rumbling of the final ferry and its wistful melody.

The dry grass, the fallen fruit, there was the rustle of cats chasing each other in the dark. It's good for Olga to be here, you've noticed it too, haven't you. That she's changed.

I WANTED TO GO to Vaporia by myself. Helena dawdled, she was picking the fruits from the ground, she seemed restless, I delayed for as long as she did and Olga was sitting in one of the lounge chairs like she used to, her toes curled over the seat, her bare legs, her slender shoulders hunched, her earphones, face in the phone and mouth open, stupidly open, moist and wonderfully open. I was anxious about leaving the two of them alone and so I waited.

The memory of my own voice: this is very secret. But at last Helena left, and I left, and Olga did not ask to come along when I left.

THE TEENS HAD STOPPED coming to the dock. The retirees didn't show up, there was no music, no talking. But the man was there, he was there when I arrived, he was sitting on the edge of the dock, and I was there, in the sun, leaned against the wall and the mountain, solo.

My swimsuit was black. An ordinary swimsuit, I'd had it for many years, it was slack on the sides with gray stretch marks, it flapped whenever I swam. This swimsuit, I thought, I was never going to wash it. I would never let it dry. I would put it in a plastic bag and when I came home I would put it on, still wet, and I would go to a public pool and swim and the sea would seep into the chlorine; through me this sea would piss into the pool, mark its territory, and I would remember what was already at this point an image, not of a particular moment but of several, melded, the image of being held by the sea, the image of the longing that had brought me here.

The man got up. He was no longer wearing his bandages, there was no white, no green. He walked back and forth on the dock the way he always did, same hesitation, same reluctance in the face of that which seemed to cause him pain. I lit a cigarette to have something to do.

The man changed his course: he was now walking straight at me. For a quivering and decisive moment I was convinced that he was coming up to me, that he was planning to say something or attack me, anything, I didn't know, anything seemed possible, and my body was tense as he walked toward me, his gaze on his injured foot, as if it were preparing itself for the encounter I had unconsciously imagined. I readied myself to hear his voice. I readied myself to say my name and ask about his.

But he walked toward me only to turn; level with the parasol he suddenly spun around and walked again, faster and smoother than before, back to the edge, from which he dived, gracefully like a swordfish and without coming up before he was already far, far out.

I CALLED JOSEF. I paused at the square in front of the city hall since my connection was bad and when I walked my footsteps on the stone made the phone rattle. I was facing the street that led to the sea, the pavement splattered by cratered bird droppings, the pigeons', and the dates that had fallen from the palm trees and onto the pavement where they lay, rotting and oozing.

He said he'd been to see Alain. He asked about you, he told me, I said you had left the country. Was it sad to see him, I asked, was it good. Josef's response was vague, like he was hiding something that had happened in my absence, not because he couldn't have told me—not out of worry that it would have made me angry, hurt—but because it didn't concern me.

I didn't know what to say to him. Standing there, holding his voice in my hand, I realized I had hoped something would happen in me when I heard him talk, but it didn't. All around me the afternoon was cooling and I stood in the same place.

I tried to tell him about the man in Vaporia but I was sloppy about it, turned it into a pointless story; I heard Josef waiting for something more but I had nothing else to say.

When are you coming home, he asked. I told him I didn't know. I'll never come home, I thought.

HELENA WASN'T at home when I got there; a relief, since I'd worried on the way back that she'd returned too early on this particular day, earlier than normal just like she had left later than normal that morning, and that she and Olga had already been alone together for a long time, and that she somehow, using one of her regular techniques—anger, fishing for a secret— had persuaded Olga to tell her something, tell her everything. I called Helena's name as I stepped through the door, I put my things away with the feigned nonchalance of a murderer, I got no answer. No Helena on the ground floor, no Helena in the sarcophagus, in the garden; no sign of Olga either.

I walked up the spiral staircase, exaggerating the noise of my steps, like a warning: come out if you're here.

Her door was shut. Mine, however, was open, which was not how I'd left it, and on the bed was Olga, face down with her head on the pillow, her arms wrapped around it. It seemed like she'd been lying like that for a very long time waiting for me, that she'd prepared this tableau. She turned around when I entered the room, her movements slow and measured; I shut the door behind me. Her face was red, swollen, wet. I sat down on the bed next to her, moving with the same calm and restraint, as if to avoid bothering or upsetting her. Suddenly everything about my body seemed too much, vulgar: my wet hair, my salty face, the clothes that chafed against the skin, the thighs that met when I sat, flesh that swelled. I didn't speak and she just looked at me for a long while, her eyes sticky and half-open, the eyes of a newborn animal.

Are you mad at me, she pleaded, finally. Everyone is

always mad at me, I can't do anything right, uhu—she collapsed in tears, prey to the violence of crying, seemingly involuntarily. Her face contorted in a desperate mask and I embraced her: no, no, no, why would I be mad at you? I kissed her hot cheeks. I held her. Her shoulders were narrow and hard, bent, shaking violently. I'm not angry. I undressed her. I towered like a giant, I was enormous, coarse, a wave that washed over her. Olga slippery under my hands, Olga's mouth open, wet tongue, wet face, her teeth bumping into mine, she was trembling, she gaped as if she were about to drink. Her body grew very still, stiff. She whimpered. I'm not mad, and she went silent.

It felt like devastation, it felt like great riches, I was consumed by them. I burned the ground she was walking on, I gave her an indelible memory, I erected a border, there would be no way back. I tore a hole in her history.

In the great silence that fell over my room, in the haze of half-slumber, timelessness, I pictured her death. Not real death, not like a photograph, but a painting. I fantasized about her throwing herself out a window, a silver spiral flung at the ground, the repetition like the picture of velocity, eight bodies, eight arms extended, like an octopus. I saw my hands around her neck, I saw her bathing in the sunlight, her irises turning honey in the light, I saw theater blood flood—no, flow calmly—out of her cleft skull, red silk ribbons.

No, she would not die like this. This was not a movie. This was not *The Children's Hour*. This was not *Dracula's Daughter*. No snare, no arrow piercing the heart, no punishment. She would keep living; I would have nothing to grieve.

6.

❧ Europa ❧

THE WORLD GOT SMALLER. DURING those days, as the sun paled and the evenings got cold and the wind more forsaken at night, I was paralyzed by my fear of leaving Olga and Helena alone. I feared using the bathroom, I listened to every sound; a muted voice drifting from the street or the screaming of the cats turned into a confession. We still ate our breakfast in the garden, the mornings were the same, long and warm, but cold came with sunset and we moved inside to the little kitchen table for dinner, we lit candles, an intense, yellow light that made the shadows sharp and threatening, the air stiflingly warm, Helena: it's almost like Christmas, we sat so close to each other around the small table that I could feel their breath, sour white wine and Olga's sweet mouth.

I couldn't go out alone anymore. I didn't dare. One day I realized I would never do it again, I would never wander as I had, without destination or purpose other than to pass the time while waiting for someone to want something from me, want me. I had seen everything I would see. I knew the end was drawing near.

The world got bigger one morning when Helena said: it's almost October, can you believe it? The months slammed into me, the year that was happening without me. Without us. This was a lost time. This was happening somewhere else. I felt nauseated when I heard her say "October."

THAT AFTERNOON, at dusk, Helena wanted us all to go look at the sunset together from the balcony in my room. She was in a frightening mood, unnervingly merry, she got a bottle of Tsipouro, a pre-drink, she said, let's do something nice together, actually it was best to be on the roof, she said, the view was better from there, but she was so scared of heights, she was too scared to climb the ladder. Hearing her talk about the roof made me feel exposed, and violated too, as if she'd trespassed on something that was mine. The site of a history she had no connection to, one that wasn't hers to know. The juxtaposition was dizzying. It made me feel sick. I remembered the prospect that had struck me in the garden, that she might learn. I remembered that nothing was mine. Everything was hers. I hated her for it.

She led the way up the stairs, Olga came next, me last. Level with my bed she paused, as if she'd caught some smell. She turned to me, past Olga: the energy in here is just so different now, you can really feel it, isn't it so cool how these things work, it doesn't feel like my room at all anymore.

We stood side by side on the narrow balcony and regarded the roofs in front of us, the antennae and the telephone lines. My only photo from that time, the picture I never sent to Josef. My sole proof. I was there.

But it was the wrong direction for the sunset, and we never saw the sun come down, only the sky darkening, a deeper blue, pink beyond the mountains, the horizon disappearing and the lights from another city on another island coming on, setting it in relief in the emptiness. I had never noticed that island before. Olga shifted from one foot to the other and looked bored. I drank from my glass with liquor, no ice; it was lukewarm and sharp. I could have sworn, Helena said, that you could see the sunset from here. Maybe you used to be able to see it, though that's impossible of course. I remembered it that way. Oh well.

And we went back down again.

HAD WE NOT already been to the sea we could have dreamed of going there. But we had nothing to dream of, and we went to the sea one last time without knowing it was the last time. The waves were tall at the farthest dock, and at the first one a couple of cats had gathered to drink rainwater from a hole in the concrete where the parasol used to be; the parasol had vanished, it had been removed at some point and we hadn't noticed. Olga was wearing a thick sweater and sat with her knees pulled to her chest, the hairs on her legs stood up, she was scratching at the ground with her nails. She didn't swim. I got in once and then I sat next to her wrapped in my towel, my hair heavy and ice-cold against my back. But the sun still warmed my skin, it warmed the ground where we sat. We watched the ferry come and go. We heard the church bells and the beating of the waves; together they created a discordant rhythm.

We weren't alone. A few people lay on the wooden deck, two older women had brought folding beach recliners and were eating something from a Tupperware container while conversing softly behind us.

Olga seemed sad and guarded. I had the sense that she was expecting me to say something to her, but I didn't know what. The clouds chased across the white sky and the air felt humid when the sun disappeared behind the dome of the church. The weather isn't great today, I said, but I'm sure it'll be better tomorrow.

WE WALKED BACK to the house, keeping the silence we'd had by the ocean, a silence that felt like a pause. I felt like I was walking alone even though she was right next to me; she was so far away and inexplicably brooding. Something was happening, I knew. But I didn't know what, and I couldn't do anything about it.

Traversing the square I noticed a group of teens on the stairs to the city hall. I thought I recognized them from the dock, though they could easily have been other kids; they all looked the same to me. The same smooth skin and long hair, the same posture, the same bounce to their bodies. Compared to us they seemed bundled up in their jeans and big sweaters and sneakers. Olga was wearing a sweater but her legs were bare. I had on my shirt with the yellowed collar, which was getting a bit smelly by now, a mixture of sweat, SPF, salt.

The kids were passing a soda bottle between themselves and it was a choreography I remembered: dodge the dregs, don't get stuck with the saliva. Their school bags were scattered all around with garish books peeking out of them. It was late afternoon, the freedom before home called with evening meals, homework, TV, before sleep called in a bed that would soon be too narrow. Infatuations that were largely fantasies. The first unrequited love. The first happy, very solemn love: this love is forever, I'll never forget you, we'll never change.

I noticed Olga glancing at them, or I thought I did. I

furtively touched her neck and she swatted my hand away. What? Nothing.

We kept walking. At the harbor she slowed down until she was walking very slowly, irritatingly slowly, as if she were testing the limits of how slowly she could move without stopping altogether. I mimicked her pace. We arrived at the house and she continued inward, upstairs; she closed the door and I showered, I poured myself a glass of wine and I waited, Helena came home, we ate dinner at the kitchen table, the wax candles, yellow light. Helena: you look like a dying duck in a thunderstorm, what's going on? Olga: nothing. She left the table with the plate still at her seat.

But in the night she came to my room. In the night I held her while she cried softly, she couldn't tell me why. All she could do was repeat, again and again, in a voice that was quiet and restrained: I have nobody, I have nobody.

A NEW SEASON ARRIVED. Once it was there it seemed like a shift that occurred in one single day even though the change had been happening for a long while. It was windy all day, the water was cold, the sky white, the cats were hiding. A cold rain was falling, dirty water and flowers came coursing down the streets and the city stairs, things dried along the walls and blew away, dust entered the foyer, the brown shells of bougainvillea that had dried and blown into the alleys.

We brought the garden chairs inside. We ate our breakfast in the kitchen. We stayed indoors all day because there was nothing else to do. Helena got restless, she was chilly, her fingers turned white. Helena with the ferry timetable: we can't stay here, I'm going crazy. Helena wanted to start working again. I heard myself plead: it might get warmer again, soon. If the wind dies down. The weather was strange, it wasn't fall but not summer either, the house never got warm. Helena with the weather report: it is going to get warmer again actually, but it would take too long. She was impatient. She was done.

She booked ferry tickets for the three of us and wanted to spend a few days with a friend in Athens; it was understood that this was where I would leave them, go back home, make the last leg of the trip alone. Olga would go with her, I would not. Olga would go with her, not with me.

I didn't know what I was returning to. The thought of going home was absurd; I didn't want to go. I wanted to stop time. I wanted to start over again, experience everything exactly the way it had been, again and again. I hated it when time ended. I hated the pace I never seemed able to slot my life into. I had been too desperate, stayed too long; I had let my chance to leave them on my own terms slip away. They would leave me. They belonged to each other. It was natural, it was something I had known all along.

But it was only when the end was given its date and shape that the vastness of my loneliness opened up, the emptiness of the future expanding infinite, enormous, and all my fantasies, my vague hopes for an intimacy that would be permanent, life-changing, left me.

THE JOURNEY TO ERMOUPOLI became a parenthesis that kept the weeks in place now that it was given a mirror in the journey back, one that would imitate it in reverse. I knew that the memory of the second journey would dilute the memory of the first; I knew that this process had already begun. I was picturing things again, events and sights that had been real turned into snapshots and memory tableaux. Days and hours blended now that I, even before I'd left the island, even before I had put this time behind me—while I was, in fact, still in the midst of it—started to think of the past weeks as one single event.

There were certain images I wanted to preserve, but whenever I fumbled in an attempt to keep them safe, hidden and distilled so that I could play them back to myself, they slipped from my grasp. I sought the complete picture, but all I found were discrete details I clung to, held up in front of me like shards.

I saw Olga's closed eyes hover in the air. I saw her knee. I saw her armpit, the neck where it turned into jaw. She was mutilated. I couldn't fit these pieces to make the person who was still where I was, this person I could still touch, whose voice I could still hear.

THE LAST NIGHT. The sea was far away; there was no longer a sea. No sun, no blue dome scaffolded. I watched the ray of light cross the floor and had sentimental thoughts: it was the last time I would see this light in this room at night, the last time I would listen to the sounds from the harbor, the horn, the ferry's jingle. But knowing it to be the last time, repeating this fact to myself, inspired no feelings. The night was too similar to all the other nights that had been followed by additional nights. The body knew nothing. The body was dragging. I was looking at the light to prepare a past.

ON THE LAST NIGHT I waited. I hadn't spoken a word to Olga all day and it reminded me of the first days after my arrival at Ermoupoli. It made it seem as if everything that had occurred in between then and now had been a dream. It turned blurry. It turned grotesque. I saw myself from the outside, my body against hers, crushing and choking. I wanted to replay everything, minute by minute, second by second. I wanted to see it all again. I wanted an assurance I couldn't get. Sensations I'd carried with me, the memory of the hands, the memory of the mouth, of the lips and the tongue, they slipped away and were replaced by pictures that were revolting. Everything seemed to have calcified and dried up and I was tormented where I lay alone, all alone as the night went on.

Had I done anything wrong? No. All I wanted was to be loved. And she had loved me, I thought, she had loved me like nobody else would be able to love me. Because it was the first love. Because she had seen me here, without context. A love story free from old grief. A young love free from memories. Free from future. I gave her a story she'd be able to tell someone who loved her later on, someone who would want to know everything about her. And she would say: I was fifteen years old, and it was summer, well, technically it was fall . . .

AT LAST I DID HEAR the footsteps on the landing. I had almost fallen asleep and the sounds of the steps, the door that closed, they startled me the way you startle when you wake from a dream about falling: it had been so close, I could have fallen asleep and woken to a new day, the day of the journey back home, when everything would be over.

She came with an apology: I wasn't able to sleep, were you. I heard the affected ease, her rehearsed delivery, and I heard myself say, in the same tone: no, me neither. Come here.

I gave her my arm just like I had so many times before and she lay down next to me, by my side, head by my neck. A hand on my belly.

And I saw, perhaps for the first time with absolute clarity, how very small she was. I didn't see her child's body, I didn't see the adult body seeking its shape, the negative space that would receive her as she swelled and grew. I saw her the way she was in that moment, in my arms, the way she had never been before and never would be again.

THE MILK IN THE SINK and the orange juice, no pulp, all of it went down the drain after breakfast. Foam swelled and spread over the stone floor. Dust and spray cleaner, a pink bottle, the scent of bread wafting through an open door elsewhere, somewhere out of sight in the neighborhood, a smell of Europe, I thought, while we mopped the floor. We: Helena and I. Olga had reverted to child again, she hid in her room or on the roof, I didn't know, her door was shut. We tossed buckets of water over the tiles in the foyer, rinsing it all out, the dust that blew in every day, and the water flowed onto the street and took all kinds of things with it: little tufts of grass in the cracks of the walls, dried flowers, fish bones the cats left behind when given leftovers on small plates, hair-thin. The sound as the water hit the ground: bam, bam.

It's always a bit sad to leave, Helena said, but she seemed excited, expectant. She was looking forward to Athens. She was looking forward to being in a big city again, you can always see the sky here, don't you get tired of it? No. I would never have tired of it. She wanted to move somewhere. Leave Sweden. She felt like having a new experience, there was always something to experience for the first time, always a place waiting for her. Just think, she said, that this house is the only anchor I've had in many years. Who would have thought. I thought this would be the place I came to get away, but it's become where I go to come home.

I asked about washing the bed linens and she said no. There was a woman who'd do it after we'd left. A woman? A neighbor. She has a key, Helena said. In the past Helena had rented the house out, but it was too much work and she didn't like knowing that other people had been in her space. There was this one couple, she said. Brits. Two men her age, maybe a bit younger. She was basically sure they were a couple. They came year after year, stayed for ten days in late summer. I can't explain it, she said, I probably sound crazy. But I couldn't bear the fact that they came back. Nobody else came back, but those two did, year after year, ten days, pretty much the same dates every year. And she imagined them telling each other, year after year, that they were coming back to *their* house, the house that was actually her house, and how something of them lingered every time they left; it bothered her.

I could picture these men. I imagined them shaving at the little mirror in the bathroom, sitting in the garden in the morning, sleeping in the same bed I'd been sleeping in at night, Helena's old bed; they had listened to the sounds I had listened to, or other sounds, too, maybe the sounds were different back then, it was a few years ago. Suddenly I had the urge to look them up and get in touch. I had the strange feeling of missing these people who, like me, had been guests in this house.

The fact that she was bothered by it was completely unrelated, Helena underscored, to the fact that they were two men. She wasn't even sure if they actually were a romantic couple. But who maintains a standing vacation like that, she said, for that long and to the same place, with a friend— two women, sure, maybe, but two men, no. They definitely weren't siblings. In any case it didn't matter, it wasn't important to her. One year they didn't get in touch about renting her house and she never heard from them again, she didn't know what had become of them, maybe they weren't even alive anymore, no clue.

She used to pay her neighbor to clean the house after the guests had left. And now, when she no longer rented the house out, she'd kept the neighbor on to wash the bed linen, check on the garden in the spring—I always want to come in the spring, she said, but it's so rare that I can make it, and you know me, I'm not exactly a handyman—and in any case it wasn't a lot of money. But when it came to cleaning, these days she preferred to clean the house herself, the ritual of it, that's what she liked, the water and the scents, rinsing it out, a form of closure.

It didn't seem like she had the same feeling about this woman, who had the key to her house, who took care of it and who had taken care of it for so long; it didn't seem like she had the same fear about her as she had of the men: that she would somehow make a mark, stay, conquer what Helena viewed as her own. This woman had no name. She had no age. I didn't know if I'd seen her in the neighborhood but I realized that she must have seen me and known which house I belonged to. That in the mind of this unknown woman, I had, for a couple of weeks in late summer or early fall, naturally belonged to this house.

I WOULD'VE LIKED to stumble on the abandoned house again, the one with the garden that resembled Helena's.

We were leaving around dinnertime and once we'd finished cleaning, once the beds were stripped and the sheets had been placed in a bag, once the bags were neatly arranged in the hall and the fridge was emptied, the rest of the day was a protracted, restless wait. Olga did not come out. She kept to her room. Helena and I sat in the kitchen, smoking and drinking coffee. The smells mixed with the cleaning soap and the slightly sour, muddy scent of the wet floor. The garden door was shut, locked, and the stone table stood beneath the pergola's stiff foliage, silent and lonely. It looked less like a table and more like a site of sacrifice, a slab where you might cut someone's throat.

Helena checked her watch, her phone. She had put her hair in a clip, which she kept taking out to pull through her hair, combing it, then clacking the clip like castanets before putting it back in again.

I didn't know if it was because of me or Helena that Olga didn't want to leave her room. Were it not for my fear of leaving them alone I would've gone out. I would have liked to see the abandoned garden. I would have liked to repeat the farewell I thought I had taken several weeks earlier, the one that wasn't a real farewell, just the staging of a farewell, a farewell that had looked nothing like this, this drawn-out, mundane wait for the moment we could leave for the ferry terminal, board the boat that would leave at a certain hour, then wait some more while the hours went by and the end, the real end, came closer. I would have liked to experience the staged version. I would have liked to see the abandoned garden in order to connect with some kind of feeling, a more definitive and satisfying feeling, more charged, than what I felt at the time.

I felt no grief sitting in the kitchen. I would have liked to feel grief. All I had was a feeling of emptiness, like a hunger, it was in my stomach. There was anxiety too, a small and ugly feeling. I didn't want to leave Olga and Helena alone.

In retrospect this fear of leaving them alone made no sense: they'd be alone together in less than twenty-four hours, they would be alone together a lot; all their lives they would be alone together without me. They wouldn't be able to escape each other. They had something that tied them together, that tied them to this world. The blood, the yearslong shared history, the history that would continue even if they severed contact, continue even if Olga at some future point spoke the words: my mom and I haven't talked in twenty years. They would have to cut ties with each other whereas I would vanish from their lives, unnoticed. I would vanish from their lives. I would vanish as I had so many times before. Not missed. I could die and they wouldn't hear about it for a long time, maybe ever.

There was a layer of sludge at the bottom of the coffee cup. In the ashtray, which we'd washed but were now using again, the gray ash had turned black in the water that hadn't dried. Helena took out her clip and pulled it through her hair, distracted. Everything was silent and congealed. There was something we weren't talking about and the air was heavy with our shared lack of knowing. She seemed irritated, but it was a different kind of irritation than the one I'd honed a keen sense for during the time I had gotten to know her, that slightly manic, focused irritation, which could suddenly transform into something else, an outburst of laughter. This time it seemed different, more obscure, thick, something that came from deep inside. It was rubbing off on me. I was not in my body. The hand that brought the cup to the mouth, the final bitter, silty mouthful, that hand was not mine.

I wanted goodbye to be in the future, in the distant future, distant from this hand and this cup, from this afternoon that wasn't a real afternoon, just interstitial time; I wanted it to be in a future where all feelings were remote and beautiful, like the stars or a person in a very old photograph. I wanted a scene.

But there was no scene, no words and no distance, and the afternoon came to an end; I washed the coffee cup and the ashtray and while I was in the kitchen and Helena was at the table Olga came down the stairs, she didn't say anything special, she said: Umm hi, and she held on to the banister, standing in between me and her mother. Helena fixed her hair atop her head. We should go, we should get there early to get good seats.

WE SHOULD HAVE LEFT while it was still light out. Helena walked with Olga and me in tow across the ferry's inside deck, the sofas, the thick windows, the cafés and the slot machines, headed to the bow and the outside deck, stacked plastic chairs. She wanted us to be outside, and the three of us sat where we could see the sea and the sky; she repeated: we should have left while it was still light out, but she didn't want to go inside. In the daytime, she said, the view from the ferry was gorgeous when it took off, the water so turquoise you wouldn't believe it, it no longer looked like water, it was the engines of the ferry that did it, the foam, it made the water around the ship look like arctic ice. But it was dark, and we saw no turquoise water and we didn't see the city lights as we departed, as the ferry left the harbor and pushed into the dark.

Olga looked unhappy. Helena's voice, loud over the roaring and vibrations of the ferry steaming ahead: I think there's a birthday coming up, she was trying to get Olga excited about it as if she were a very young child. So we never made it to Delos, she shouted at me. The sound of the ferry was drowning her out, another time . . . the ruins . . . there's time, they've been there for thousands of . . . but she knew just as well as I did that there would be no second time, and I knew that the excursion we were about to put out of reach was something she'd keep talking about, with Olga, with others, she'd bring it up again and again without ever actually doing it. Maybe there was something about it that worried her though she didn't know it. Not about seeing the place again, but about seeing the person she'd been the first time she saw it, or worse: not seeing that person. To understand that what was gone was lost forever and had left no trace behind. Perhaps it was anxiety in the face of what endures over millennia and what does not endure.

I could really go for a beer right now, she said, usually I never drink beer, but this is a good occasion for a beer, a beer right now would be incredible, do you want one? She stretched the question, made it way too long, I said: yeah, I'd love one, and she kept providing her motivations, this beer, an ice-cold beer, to drink it from a plastic glass or maybe straight from the bottle, that's something special, normally I don't—I couldn't hear her well and I heard myself repeat over and over, yeah, yeah, definitely, totally, while Olga stared into space with an expression of mordant scorn. It was a horrible situation. At last Helena got up and I watched her leave, her waddling walk, the broad torso, the short legs.

I looked at Olga. She kept staring straight ahead. Her hands were in the pocket of her hoodie. I wanted to say something but I didn't know what, and there was nothing I could say without shouting to overpower the roar of the engine. I wanted her to look at me. I wanted her to seek something in me. I wanted to mention a feeling in order to bring it about. A memory: do you remember when—, I'll never forget when—. But I didn't say anything, and she didn't look at me, and Helena came back and gave me a tall green bottle to drink from.

Oh, she shouted at Olga, I forgot to ask if you wanted something? Want me to go back? A coke? A cup of tea, perhaps? Are you cold? Her voice was flat and nasal when she raised it. Olga said something but I couldn't hear what, I just saw her move her lips, and apparently Helena didn't hear her either because she leaned over me: what's that? Olga: no! She pulled up her shoulders, buried her neck in the hood. She slouched in the chair and stretched her legs out. At this, all three of us turned to look straight ahead. We were silent.

The ferry was going to take almost four hours. Then the subway trip, we'd be together for some of it, me heading to the last flight of the day, them to Helena's friend who was already waiting for them, who'd maybe prepared for their arrival the way Helena had once prepared for mine: making a bed or setting up the couch, preparing a late dinner. They would get off at their stop, with their bags. The doors would automatically close behind them. Nothing unusual about it. No more dramatic than saying goodbye to someone you'll see again soon. No time for it. It would be a question of minutes.

And then, I imagined, Helena might write to me, or I would write to her. Almost as soon as the doors had closed. Wishing them safe travels, thank her for everything. No. I would not write to her. I would wait for her to write. Later, maybe, it would truly be over. Their lives would keep unfolding without me. They would come back without me. Maybe they would talk about me sometimes: a guest who stayed one fall. Do you remember her.

It would always be possible to get in touch again. There would never be a real ending. Never a real boundary. I wanted the feeling to be bigger. I always wanted the feeling to be bigger.

IT WAS THERE, sitting on the ferry, sitting in between Helena and Olga in the darkness, that a particular image came back to me, the assumptions I'd made before I got there, and before they got there too, in late summer, the scenes I'd imagined when Helena told me that they were leaving, when I'd felt so alone, when I pictured her in her house at night, also alone.

They were not the same images. It was impossible to recover those images. They were lost. Instead these were new images, a new version of the weeks that had passed before I got there, a time I hadn't thought about in a long while. In this version I pictured Olga clearly, where previously I hadn't been able to see her. I saw her silence. I saw her at the table, facing Helena. I saw her in my chair. I saw her on the roof. I saw Helena's outbursts: you never want to do anything, you're so boring. I saw her eat with cautious mouthfuls. I saw her lonely summer holiday, which was no longer a summer holiday but a strange time with no beginning or end, a dreamtime. I saw her hand flit across her forehead to move a strand of hair that was no longer there. I saw her alone in the garden. I saw her alone, interminably alone, impenetrably alone.

I saw my own loneliness in her. I saw myself in her. I grieved the fantasies that left me as we traveled through the dark.

THE THREE OF US were sitting side by side, Olga, me, Helena. They had their names and their boundaries, mother and daughter. I had nothing. I was a stranger. I remained a stranger. I would vanish as strangers do. I had already begun to vanish.

I returned to the square at night. I returned to the image of the three of us, sitting the way we did now, beneath the arches, in the dark sultry evening some distance from the stage, on the outskirts of the crowd. It was cold on the ferry, but I was back in the warm night. My fingers were stiff. I was back, looking at the palm tree, which was level with my eyes, I was huge. I was a giant. I saw everything from the outside and from above. I saw the teens on the square, saw them like ants. I saw their lives stretch before them and trail them like tails, childhood memories, summer memories, memories that appeared as one body but were in fact many events that had folded together, piled up. The impulses and the recollections of particular flavors and feelings. To bite into an ice cube. To be held by the sea.

In reality there was a beginning and an end. In memory there was only this square and this night, infinite, constant. I saw Olga turn around and look at me, by the sea. By Helena's side. And I saw my own face, hiding nothing. I saw what she saw. I saw myself following her, pursuing her, through life.

I was no longer in my own body. I was in the story I was telling myself. I was preparing a memory for later.

For three days on the square they'd been showing the

world championships in harpoon fishing on a screen in front of the city hall. And there was a thunderstorm, a couple of nights later there was a thunderstorm.

That's how it happened.

Acknowledgments

I would like to thank my Swedish editor, Lisa Lindberg, for our conversations, for her guidance, and for being such a perceptive and sensitive reader.

© Evelina Boberg

HANNA JOHANSSON is a Swedish writer and critic who writes on such topics as art, literature, and queer issues. *Antiquity*, her debut novel, won the 2021 Katapultpris and was short-listed for the Borås Tidning Debutant Prize.

KIRA JOSEFSSON is a writer and translator working between English and Swedish. The winner of a PEN/Heim grant, she translates contemporary Swedish fiction and poetry, and regularly writes on U.S. events and politics in the Swedish press.